The Twins  KU-714-032

This is the first book in
Enid Blyton's wonderful
St Clare's school series

This Armada book belongs to:

_____

_____

_____

Enid Blyton

The Twins at
St Clare's

ARMADA

First published in the UK in 1941
by Methuen & Co. Ltd
Republished by Dragon Books in 1967
First published in Armada in 1988
This impression 1988

Armada is an imprint of
the Children's Division, part of
the Collins Publishing Group,
8 Grafton Street, London W1X 3LA

Printed and bound in Great Britain by
William Collins Sons & Co. Ltd, Glasgow

The Twins Make Up Their Minds

One sunny summer afternoon four girls sat on the grass by a tennis-court, drinking lemonade. Their rackets lay beside them, and the six white balls were scattered over the court.

Two of the girls were twins. Isabel and Patricia O'Sullivan were so alike that only a few people could tell which was Pat and which was Isabel. Both girls had dark brown wavy hair, deep blue eyes and a merry smile, and the Irish lilt in their voices was very pleasant to hear.

The twins were staying for two weeks with friends of theirs, Mary and Frances Waters. The four girls were talking, and Pat was frowning as she spoke. She took up her racket and banged it hard on the grass.

"It's just too bad that Mummy won't let us go to the same school as you, now that we have all left Redroofs School together. We've been friends so long – and now we've got to go to a different school, and we shan't see each other for ages."

"It's a pity that Redroofs only takes girls up to fourteen," said Isabel. "We could have stayed on together and it would have been fun. I loved being head-girl with Pat the last year – and it was fun being tennis-captain, and Pat being hockey-captain. Now we've got to go to another school that doesn't sound a bit nice – and begin at the bottom! We'll be the young ones of the school instead of head-girls."

"I do wish you were coming to Ringmere School with us!" said Frances. "It's such a nice *exclusive* school, our mother says. *You* know – only girls of rich parents, very well-bred, go there, and you make such nice friends.

We have a bedroom to ourselves and our own study, and we have to wear evening dress at night, and they say the food is wonderful!"

"And we are going to St. Clare's, where anybody can go, and the dormitories take six or eight girls and aren't nearly as nicely furnished as the maids' bedrooms are at home!" said Pat in a disgusted voice.

"I can't imagine why Mummy made up her mind to send us there instead of to Ringmere," said Isabel. "I wonder if she has *quite* decided. We're going home to-morrow and we'll both do our very very best to make her say we can go to Ringmere, Mary and Frances! We'll ring you up in the evening and tell you."

"We'll jump for joy if you have good news," said Mary. "After all, when you've been head-girls at a marvellous school like Redroofs, and had your own lovely bedroom and the best study with the best view, and a hundred girls looking up to you, it's awful to have to start again in a school you don't want to go to a bit!"

"Well, do your best to make your parents change their minds," said Frances. "Come on – let's have another set before tea!"

They all jumped up and tossed for partners. Isabel was a splendid player, and had won the tennis championship at Redroofs. She was really rather proud of her game. Pat was nearly as good, but much preferred hockey.

"They don't play hockey at St. Clare's, they play lacrosse," said Pat, dismally. "Silly game, lacrosse – playing with nets on sticks, and catching a ball all the time instead of hitting it! That's another thing I'll tell Mummy – that I don't want to play lacrosse after being hockey-captain."

The twins thought hard of all the reasons they would put before their parents when they got home the next day. They talked about it as they went home in the train.

"I'll say this, and you say that," said Pat. "After all, *we* ought to know the kind of school that would be best for us – and St. Clare's does sound too fierce for words!"

So the next evening the girls began to air their thoughts about schools. Pat began, and, as was her way, she attacked at once.

"Mummy and Daddy!" she said. "Isabel and I have been thinking a lot about what school we're to go to next, and, please, we don't want to go to St. Clare's. Every one says it's an awful school."

Their mother laughed, and their father put down his paper in surprise.

"Don't be silly, Pat," said Mrs. O'Sullivan. "It's a splendid school."

"Have you quite decided about it?" asked Isabel.

"Not absolutely," said her mother. "But Daddy and I both think it will be the best school for you now. We do think that Redroofs spoilt you a bit, you know – it's a very expensive and luxurious school, and nowadays we have to learn to live much more simply. St. Clare's is really a very sensible sort of school, and I know the Head and like her."

Pat groaned. "A sensible school! How I do hate sensible things – they're always horrid and ugly and stupid and uncomfortable! Oh, Mummy – do let us go to Ringmere School with Mary and Frances."

"Certainly not!" said Mrs. O'Sullivan at once. "It's a very snobbish school, and I'm not going to have you two girls coming home and turning up your noses at everything and everybody."

"We wouldn't," said Isabel, frowning at Pat to make her stop arguing for a while. Pat lost her temper very easily, and that didn't do when their father was there. "Mummy dear – be a pet – just let's try at Ringmere for a term or two, and then, if you think we're turning into snobs, you can take us away. But you might let us try.

They play hockey there, and we do so like that. We'd hate to have to learn a new game, just when we've got so good at hockey."

Mr. O'Sullivan rapped with his pipe on the table. "My dear Isabel, it will be good for you to start at the beginning again, and learn something new! I've thought the last year that both you girls have become very conceited, and thought far too much of yourselves. If you have to learn new things, and find you're not so wonderful as you thought you were, it will be very good for you both!"

The twins went red. They were angry and hurt and almost ready to cry. Mrs. O'Sullivan felt sorry for them.

"Daddy doesn't mean to be unkind," she said. "But he is quite right, my dears. You've had a wonderful time at Redroofs, had things all your own way, been head-girls and captains, and really lived in luxury. Now you must show us what kind of stuff you are made of when you have to start as youngsters of fourteen and a half in a school where the top classes are eighteen years old!"

Pat looked sulky. Isabel's chin shook as she answered.

"We shan't be happy, and we shan't try to be!" she said.

"Very well. Be *un*happy!" said their father, sternly. "If that's the sort of silly attitude you've learnt at Redroofs, I'm sorry we let you stay there so long. I wanted to take you away two years ago, but you begged so hard to stay, that I didn't. Now say no more about it. I shall write to St. Clare's myself tonight and enter you for next term. If you want to make me proud of you, you will cheer up and make up your minds to be good and hardworking and happy at your next school."

Their father lighted his pipe and began to read his paper again. Their mother took up her sewing. There was no more to be said. The twins left the room together and went into the garden. They found their own secret

8

place behind the thick old yew-hedge and flung themselves down on the ground. The evening sun threw its slanting golden rays around them, and they blinked in its brightness. Tears shone in Isabel's eyes.

"I never thought Mummy and Daddy would be so hard," she said. "Never!"

"After all, *we* ought to have some say in the matter," said Pat, furiously. She took a stick and dug it hard into the ground. "I wish we could run away!"

"Don't be silly," said Isabel. "You know we can't. Anyway, it's cowardly to run away. We'll have to go to St. Clare's. But how I shall hate it."

"We'll both hate it," said Pat. "And what's more, I'm jolly well going to turn up my nose at everything there! *I'm* not going to let them think we're babies of fourteen, just come from some silly prep school. I'll soon let them know that we were head-girls, and tennis- and hockey-captains. How horrid of Daddy to say we are conceited! We're not a bit. We can't help knowing that we're good at nearly everything, besides being pretty and quite amusing."

"It *does* sound a bit conceited when you talk like that," said Isabel. "We'd better not say too much when we get to St. Clare's."

"I'm going to say all I like, and you must back me up," said Pat. "People are going to know who we are, and what we can do! All the mistresses are going to sit up and take notice of us too. The O'Sullivan twins are going to be SOMEBODIES! And don't you forget it, Isabel."

Isabel nodded her dark head with its black waves of hair. "I won't forget it," she said. "I'll back you up. My word, St. Clare's will get a few surprises next term!"

The Twins Arrive At St. Clare's

The time soon came when the twins had to leave for the winter term at St. Clare's. Their mother had had a list of things they were to take with them, and the twins examined it carefully.

"It's not nearly such a long list as we had for Redroofs," said Pat. "And golly – how few dresses we are allowed! Mary and Frances said that they were allowed to take as many frocks as they liked to Ringmere – and they had both got long evening dresses like their mother! Won't they show off to us when they see us again!"

"And look – lacrosse-sticks instead of hockey-sticks!" said Isabel in disgust. "They might at least play hockey as *well* as lacrosse! I didn't even bother to *look* at the lacrosse sticks Mummy bought for us, did you? And look – we are even told what to bring in our tuck boxes! We could take what we liked to Redroofs."

"Just wait till we get to St. Clare's. We'll show that we can do as we like," said Pat. "What time is the train tomorrow?"

"Ten o'clock from Paddington," said Isabel. "Well – we shall get our first glimpse of the St. Clare girls there. I bet they'll be a queer-looking crowd!"

Mrs. O'Sullivan took the twins to London. They taxied to Paddington Station, and looked for the St. Clare train. There it was, drawn up at the platform, labelled St. Clare. On the platform were scores of girls, talking excitedly to one another, saying good-bye to their parents, hailing mistresses, and buying bars of chocolate from the tea-wagons.

A simply-dressed mistress came up to the twins. She knew that they were St. Clare girls because they had on the grey coats that were the uniform of the school. She smiled at Mrs. O'Sullivan, and looked at the list in her hand.

"These are new girls," she said, "and I am sure they must be Patricia and Isabel O'Sullivan, because they are so exactly alike. I'm your form-mistress, Miss Roberts, and I'm very pleased to see you."

This was a nice welcome and the twins liked the look of Miss Roberts. She was young and good-looking, tall and smiling – but she had a firm mouth and both Pat and Isabel felt sure that she wouldn't stand much nonsense from her form!

"Your carriage is over here, with the rest of your form," said Miss Roberts. "Say good-bye now, and get in. The train will be going in two minutes."

She went off to talk to some one else and the twins hugged their mother. "Good-bye," said Mrs. O'Sullivan. "Do your best this term, and I do hope you'll be happy at your new school. Write to me soon."

The twins got into a carriage where three or four other girls were already sitting and chattering. They said nothing, but looked with interest at the scores of girls passing by their compartment to their places farther up the train.

At their last school the twins had been the oldest and biggest there – but now they were among the youngest! At Redroofs all the girls had looked at Pat and Isabel with awe and admiration – the two wonderful head-girls – but now the twins were looking at others in the same way! Tall, dignified girls from the top form walked by, talking. Merry-voiced girls from other forms ran to get their places, calling out to one another. Younger ones scrambled into the carriages as the guard went along to warn one that the train was about to go.

The journey was quite fun. Every one had packets of sandwiches to eat at half-past twelve, and the train steward brought bottles of ginger-beer and lemonade, and cups of tea. At half-past two the train drew in at a little platform. A big notice said "Alight here for St. Clare's School".

There were big school-coaches waiting outside and the girls piled themselves in them, chattering and laughing. One of them turned to Pat and Isabel.

"There's the school, look! Up on that hill there!"

The twins looked. They saw a pleasant white building, built of large white stones, with two towers, one at each end. It looked down into the valley, over big playing-fields and gardens.

"Not nearly so nice as Redroofs," said Pat to Isabel. "Do you remember how sweet our old school used to look in the evening sun?" Its red roof was glowing, and it looked warm and welcoming – not cold and white like St. Clare's."

For a few minutes both girls were homesick for their old school and their old friends. They knew nobody at St. Clare's at all. They couldn't call out "Hallo, there!" to every one as they had done each term before. They didn't like the look of any of the girls, who seemed much more noisy and boisterous than the ones at Redroofs. It was all horrid.

"Anyway, we are lucky to have got each other," said Isabel to Pat. "I would have hated to come here all alone. Nobody seems to talk to us at all."

It was the twins' own fault, if they had but known it. They both looked "stuck-up" as one girl whispered to another. Nobody felt much inclined to talk to them or make friends.

There was the same rush of unpacking and settling in as there is at all boarding-schools. The big dormitories were full of girls putting away their things, hanging up their dresses and putting photographs out on their little dressing-tables.

There were a good many dormitories at St. Clare's. Pat and Isabel were in number 7, where there were eight white beds, all exactly alike. Each was in its own cubicle surrounded by curtains that could be drawn open or closed, just as the girls pleased. Pat's bed was next to Isabel's, much to their joy.

When the girls had unpacked a tall girl came into the dormitory calling out, "Any new girls here?"

Pat and Isabel nodded their heads. "We are new," said Pat.

"Hallo, twins!" said the tall girl, smiling, as she looked at the two sisters so exactly alike, "Are you Patricia and Isabel O'Sullivan? Matron wants to see you."

Pat and Isabel went with the girl to where the school matron sat in her comfortable room, surrounded by cupboards, chests and shelves. She was a fat, jolly-looking person, but her eyes were very sharp indeed.

"You can't deceive Matron over anything," whispered their guide. "Keep in her good books if you can."

Matron checked over sheets, towels and clothes with them. "You will be responsible for mending all your own belongings," she said.

"Good gracious!" said Pat. "There were sewing maids at our other school to do that."

"Shocking!" said Matron, briskly. "Well, there are no sewing-maids here. So be careful of your things, and remember that they cost your parents money."

"Our parents don't need to worry about torn clothes," began Pat. "Why, once at Redroofs I got caught in some barbed wire, and everything I had on was torn to bits. They were so torn that the sewing-maid said she couldn't mend a thing, and . . ."

"Well, I would have made you mend every hole, every rent, every tear," said Matron, her eyes beginning to

13

sparkle. "There's one thing I can't bear, and that's carelessness and waste. Now mind you . . . What is it, Millicent?"

Another girl had come into the room with a pile of towels, and the twins were very glad that Matron's attention was no longer given to them. They slipped out of the room quietly.

"I don't like Matron," said Pat. "And I've a jolly good mind to tear something so badly that it can't be mended, and that would give her something to think about!"

"Let's go and see what the school is like," said Isabel, slipping her arm into Pat's. "It seems much barer and colder somehow than dear old Redroofs."

The twins began to explore. The classrooms seemed much the same as any classrooms, and the view from the windows was magnificent. The twins peeped into the studies. At their old school they had shared a fine study between them, but here there were no studies except for the top form girls and the fifth form. The younger girls shared a big common room, where there was a wireless, a gramophone and a big library of books. Shelves ran round the common room and each girl shared part of a shelf, putting her belongings there, and keeping them tidy.

There were small music rooms for practising, a fine art room, an enormous gym, which was also used for assembly and concerts, and a good laboratory. The mistresses had two common rooms and their own bedrooms, and the Head lived in a small wing by herself, having her own bedroom in one of the towers, and a beautiful drawing-room below.

"It's not so bad," said Pat, after they had explored everywhere. "And the playing-fields are fine. There are many more tennis courts here than Redroofs – but of course it's a much bigger school."

"I don't like big schools," said Isabel. "I like smaller

14

schools, where you are somebody, not just a little nobody tucked away among heaps of others!"

They went into the common room. The wireless was on and a dance-band was playing cheerful music, which was almost drowned by the chatter of the girls. Some of them looked up as Pat and Isabel came in.

"Hallo, twins!" said a cheeky-looking girl with curly golden hair. "Which is which?"

"I'm Patricia O'Sullivan and my twin sister is Isabel," said Pat.

"Well, welcome to St. Clare's," said the girl. "I'm Hilary Wentworth, and you're in the same dormitory as I am. Have you been to boarding-school before?"

"Of course," said Pat. "We went to Redroofs."

"The school for snobs!" said a dark-haired girl, looking up. "My cousin went there – and didn't she fancy herself when she came home! Expected to be waited on hand and foot, and couldn't even bear to sew a button on a shoe!"

"Shut up," said Hilary, seeing that Pat went red. "You always talk too much, Janet. Well, Patricia and Isabel, this isn't the same kind of school as Redroofs – we work hard and play hard here, and we're jolly well taught to be independent and responsible!"

"We didn't want to come here," said Pat. "We wanted to go to Ringmere School, where our friends were going. Nobody thought much of St. Clare's at Redroofs."

"Dear, dear, dear, is that so?" said Janet, raising her eyebrows till they were almost lost in the dark hair on her forehead. "Well, the point is, my dear twins – not what you think of St. Clare's – but what St. Clare's thinks of *you*! Quite a different thing. Personally, I think it's a pity that you didn't go somewhere else. I've a feeling you won't fit in here."

"Janet, do be quiet," said Hilary. "It's not fair to say things like that to new girls. Let them settle in. Come on, Patricia – come on, Isabel – I'll show you the way to the Head's room. You'll have to go and say how-do-you-do to her before supper."

Pat and Isabel were almost boiling over with rage at what dark-haired Janet had said. Hilary pushed the twins out of the room. "Don't take too much notice of Janet," she said. "She always says exactly what she thinks, which is very nice when she thinks complimentary things about people, but not so good when she doesn't. You'll get used to her."

"I hope we shan't," said Pat stiffly. "I like good manners, something that was taught at our school anyway, even if it's not known here!"

"Oh, don't be stuffy," said Hilary. "Look, that's the Head's room. Knock on the door first – and try some of your good manners on Miss Theobald!"

The twins knocked on the door. A pleasant, rather deep voice called "Come in!" Pat opened the door and the twins went in.

The Head Mistress was sitting at her desk, writing. She looked up and smiled at the girls.

"I needn't ask who you are," she said. "You are so alike that you must be the O'Sullivan twins!"

"Yes," said the girls, looking at their new Head Mistress. She was grey-haired, with a dignified, serious face that broke into a lovely smile at times. She shook hands with each twin.

"I am very glad to welcome you to St. Clare's," she said. "I hope that one day we shall be proud of you. Do your best for us and St. Clare's will be able to do its best for you!"

"We'll try," said Isabel, and then was quite surprised at herself to find that she had said that. She didn't mean to try at all! She looked at Pat. Pat said nothing but stared straight in front of her.

"I know your mother quite well," said Miss Theobald.

16

"I was glad when she decided to send you here. You must tell her that when you write to her, and give her my kind regards."

"Yes, Miss Theobald," said Pat. The Head Mistress nodded at them with a smile, and turned to her desk again.

"What funny children!" she thought to herself. "Anyone might think they hated to be here! Perhaps they are just shy or homesick."

But they were neither shy nor homesick. They were just two obstinate girls determined to make the worst of things because they hadn't been sent to the school of their choice!

A Bad Beginning

The twins soon found that St. Clare's was quite different from their old school. Even the beds were not nearly so comfortable! And instead of being allowed to have their own pretty bedspreads and eiderdowns to match, every girl had to have the same.

"I hate being the same as everyone else!" said Pat. "Goodness – if only we were allowed to have what we liked, wouldn't we make everyone stare!"

"What I hate most is being one of the young ones," said Isabel, dismally. "I hate being spoken to as if I were about six, when the top form or fifth-form girls say anything to me. It's 'Here, you – get out of my way! Hi, you! Fetch me a book from the library!' It's just too bad."

The standard of work was higher at St. Clare's than at most schools, and although the twins had good brains, they found that they were rather behind their form in many ways, and this, too, annoyed them very much. They had so hoped that they would impress the others in so many ways – and it seemed as if they were even less than nobodies!

They soon got to know the girls in their form. Hilary Wentworth was one and the sharp-tongued Janet Robins. Then there was a quiet, straight-haired girl called Vera Johns and a rather haughty-looking girl called Sheila Naylor, whose manners were very arrogant. The twins didn't like her at all.

"I don't know what she's got to be so haughty about!" said Pat to Isabel. "It's true she's got a lovely home because I've seen a photo of it on her dressing-table – but my goodness, she sometimes talks like our parlourmaid at home. Then she seems to remember she mustn't talk like that and goes all haughty and silly."

Then there was Kathleen Gregory, a frightened looking girl of fifteen, who was the only one who really tried to make friends with the twins the first week. Most of the other girls left them alone, except for being polite, and telling them the ways of the school. They all thought that Pat and Isabel were very "stuck-up".

"Kathleen is funny," said Isabel. "She seems so eager to make friends with us, and lend us books and shares her sweets. She's been at St. Clare's for a year, and she doesn't seem to have any friends at all. She keeps asking me to walk with her when we go out, and I keep saying I can't because I've got you."

"I feel rather sorry for her somehow," said Pat. "She reminds me of a lost dog trying to find a new master!"

Isabel laughed. "Yes, that's just it! I think of all the girls that I like Hilary the best in our form. She's so natural and jolly – a real sport."

The twins were very much in awe of the older girls, who seemed very grown-up to them. The top form especially seemed almost as old and even more dignified than the mistresses! The head-girl, Winifred James, spoke a few words to the twins the first week. She was a tall, clever-looking girl with pale blue eyes and pretty soft hair. St. Clare's was proud of her, for she had passed many difficult exams. with flying colours.

"You are the new girls, aren't you?" she said. "Settle in and do your best. Come to me if you are in any difficulty. I'm the head-girl and I should like to help you if ever I can."

"Oh, thank you," said the twins, feeling quite overcome at being addressed by the head-girl. Winifred went off with her friends, and the twins stared after her.

"She's rather nice," said Isabel. "In fact, I think most of the top form girls are nice, though they're awfully serious and proper."

They liked their form-mistress, Miss Roberts, too, though she would stand no nonsense at all. Sometimes Pat would try to argue about something, and say, "Well, that's what I was taught at my old school!"

Then Miss Roberts would say, "Really? Well, do it that way if you like – but you won't get very far up your form! Do remember that what suits one school won't work in another. Still, if you like to be obstinate, that's your own look-out!"

Then Pat would stick out her lower lip, and Isabel would go red, and the rest of the form would smile to itself. Those "stuck-up" girls were having to learn a lesson!

The art-mistress, Miss Walker, was a merry soul, young and jolly, and very good at her work. She was pleased to find that both twins could draw and paint well. Pat and Isabel loved Miss Walker's classes. They were very go-as-you-please, much more like their old school. The girls were allowed to chatter and laugh as they worked, and it was often a very noisy class indeed.

Mam'zelle was not so easy-going. She was very strict, elderly, conscientious and fierce. She wore pince-nez glasses on her nose, and these were always slipping off when she was cross, which was fairly often. She had

19

enormous feet, and a rather harsh voice that the twins hated at first. But Mam'zelle had also a great sense of fun, and if anything tickled her she would go off into enormous roars of laughter that set the whole class laughing too.

Pat and Isabel came up against Mam'zelle very much at first, for although they could speak and understand French quite well, they had never bothered very much about French grammar and rules. And Mam'zelle bothered a great deal about those!

"You girls, Patricia and Isabel!" she cried. "It is not enough to speak my language! You write it abominably! See this essay – it is abominable, abominable!"

"Abominable" was Mam'zelle's favourite adjective. She used it for everything – the weather, a broken pencil, the girls, and her own eye-glasses when they slipped off her big nose! Pat and Isabel called her "Mam'zelle Abominable" between themselves, and were secretly more than a little afraid of the loud-voiced, good-hearted big French-woman.

History was taken throughout the school by Miss Kennedy, and her classes were a riot. Poor Miss Kennedy was a frump, and could not manage any class of girls for more than five minutes. She was nervous and serious, always tremendously polite, listened to every question that was put to her no matter how silly, and explained every difficulty at great length. She never seemed to see that half the time the girls were pulling her leg.

"Before Miss Kennedy came we had her friend Miss Lewis," said Hilary to the twins. "She was marvellous. Then she fell ill in the middle of last term, and asked the Head to have her friend, Miss Kennedy, until she was well enough to come back. Old Kenny has got umpteen degrees, and is supposed to be even cleverer than the Head – but my word, she's a goose!"

Bit by bit the twins sorted out the various girls and

mistresses, grew to know the classes and the customs of the school, and settled in. But even when two weeks had gone by they had not got used to being "nobodies instead of somebodies" as Pat complained.

One thing they found most annoying. It was the custom at St. Clare's for the younger girls to wait on the two top forms. The fifth- and sixth-form girls shared studies, two friends having a study between them.

They were allowed to furnish these studies themselves, very simply, and, in cold weather, to have their own fire there, and to have tea by themselves instead of in the hall with the others.

One day a girl came into the common room where the twins were reading and called to Janet, "Hi, Janet – Kay Longden wants you. You're to light her fire and make some toast for her."

Janet got up without a word and went out. Pat and Isabel stared after her in surprise.

"Golly! What cheek of Kay Longden to send a message to Janet like that! I'm jolly sure I wouldn't go and light anybody's fire!" said Pat.

"And neither would I!" said Isabel. "Let one of the maids light it – or Kay herself."

Hilary Wentworth looked up from her embroidery. "It will be your turn next!" she said. "Look out next week for sudden messages, twins. If the fifth or sixth want anything doing, they expect us to do it. It's the custom of the school – and anyway, it doesn't hurt us. We can have our turn at sending messages and ordering the lower forms about when we're top-formers ourselves!"

"I never heard of such a thing!" cried Pat, furiously. "I jolly well won't go and do a thing for any one. Our parents didn't send us here to wait on lazy top-formers. Let them light their own fires and make their own toast! Isabel and I won't do a thing! And they can't make us either!"

"Hoity-toity!" said Hilary. "I never knew such a hot temper. Get further away from me, Pat, you're scorching me!"

Pat slammed down her book and flounced out of the room. Isabel followed her. All the other girls laughed.

"Idiots!" said Hilary. "Who do they think they are, anyway? Why don't they get some sense? They wouldn't be at all bad if only they would shake down. I vote we knock some of their corners off, else we shall hate them like anything!"

"O.K.," said Vera. "I'm willing. I say, what a shock for them when they find they've got to wait on the top-formers too. I hope they get Belinda Towers. I had to wait on her last term, and my word, didn't she make me skip around! She got it into her head that I was lazy, and I'm sure I lost a whole stone rushing round in circles after her one week!"

The girls laughed. Sheila Naylor spoke haughtily. "The worst of people who think they are somebodies is that so often they are just nobodies. I'm sure I shouldn't even trouble to *know* Patricia and Isabel at home."

"Oh, come off the high horse, Sheila," said Hilary. "The twins aren't as bad as all that. Anyway, there are a few shocks in store for them!"

So there were – and they came the very next week!

A Little Trouble For The Twins

One day, about half-past five, when the twins were writing home, one of the fourth-formers popped her head in at the door.

"Hi, there!" she said. "Where are the O'Sullivan twins? Belinda Towers wants one of them."

Pat and Isabel looked up. Pat went red. "What does

22

she want us for?" she asked.

."How should I know?" said the messenger. "She's been out over the fields this afternoon, so maybe she wants her boots cleaned. Anyway, jump to it, or you'll get into a row!"

The messenger disappeared. The twins sat still. Hilary looked at them.

"Go on, idiots," she said. "One of you must go and find out what Belinda wants. Don't keep her waiting, for goodness' sake. She's got about as hot a temper as you have, Pat."

"I'll go," said Isabel, and got up. But Pat pulled her down.

"No, don't," she said. "I'm not going to clean anybody's boots! And you're not, either."

"Look here, Pat, don't be goofy," said Janet. "Belinda may want to tell you something. Golly, she might want to ask you if you'll play in a match. She's captain, you know."

"Oh," said Pat. "Well, I shouldn't think it's that because neither Isabel nor I have ever played lacrosse before, and we were pretty bad at it yesterday."

"Well, do GO!" said Hilary. "You've got to go in the end, so why not go now?"

Another girl popped her head in at the door. "I say! Belinda's foaming at the mouth! Where *are* those O'Sullivan twins? They'll get it hot if one of them doesn't go along!"

"Come on," said Pat to Isabel. "We'll go and see what she wants. But I'm not doing any boot-cleaning or fire-lighting, that's certain. And neither are you!"

The two got up and went out of the room. Everybody giggled. "Wish I could go and see what happens!" said Janet. "I love to see Belinda in a rage!"

Belinda Towers was in her study with Pamela Harrison, the girl who shared it with her. Pat opened the door.

23

"Knock, can't you!" cried Belinda. "Barging in like that! And I should jolly well like to know why you've been all this time coming. I sent for you ages ago."

Pat was rather taken aback, and Isabel did not dare to say anything.

"Well, haven't you a tongue between you?" said Belinda. "My goodness, Pam, did you ever see such a pair of boobs? Well, as you've *both* come, you can both do a spot of work for me, I want my boots cleaned and Pam's too. And make up my fire for me and put the kettle on to boil. You'll find water just down the passage. Come on, Pam – we'll go and collect our prep and by that time the kettle will be boiling and we'll make tea."

The two big girls walked to the door. Pat, very red and angry, stopped them.

"I didn't come to St. Clare's to wait on the older girls," she said. "Neither did my twin. We shan't clean your boots nor put on the kettle, nor make up the fire."

Belinda stopped as if she had been shot. She stared at Pat as if she was some particularly nasty insect. Then she turned to Pam.

"Did you hear that?" she said. "Talk about cheek! All right, my girl – no walks down the town for you. Just remember that!"

The twins stared at Belinda in dismay. The St. Clare girls were allowed to go down to the town in twos to buy anything they needed, or to look at the shops, or even to go to the cinema if they had permission. Surely Belinda hadn't the power to stop them doing that?

"I don't think you've any right to say that," said Pat. "I shall go to Winifred James and tell her what you've said and ask her about it."

"Well, I'm blessed!" said Belinda, flaring up angrily, her red hair seeming to flame too. "You *do* want taking down a peg, don't you? Run off to Winifred, by all means. Tell your little tales and see what happens."

24

Pat and Isabel went out of the study. Isabel was very much upset, and wanted to stay and do what Belinda had ordered, but Pat was furious. She took hold of her twin's arm and marched her off to Winifred's study. The head-girl had her own study, which she shared with no one. Pat dared not go in without knocking. So, she knocked quietly.

"Come in!" said Winifred's voice. The twins went in. Winifred was working at a table, "What is it?" she said. "I'm rather busy."

"Please, Winifred," said Pat, "Belinda Towers ordered us to clean her boots, make up her fire and put her kettle on. And when we said we wouldn't she said we weren't to go down into the town. So we've come to ask you about it."

"I see," said Winifred. "Well, it's the custom of this school to get the juniors to wait on the seniors within reason. It doesn't hurt them. When you go to Rome, you must do as Rome does, you know."

"But we didn't want to come to St. Clare's, so we don't want to follow silly customs of that sort," said Pat. "Do we, Isabel?"

Isabel shook her head. She couldn't think how Pat could dare to speak to Winifred like that. Her knees were shaking as she stood! She was never so brave as Pat.

"I think I should wait a little while before you call our customs silly," said Winifred. "Now listen — can't you clean boots? Don't you know how to make up a fire? Have you never put a kettle on to boil?"

"We never had to at Redroofs," said Pat, obstinately. "And we don't at home either."

"I don't think I'd know how to clean muddy boots!" said Isabel, thinking that perhaps if she said that, Winifred would let them off.

"Good heavens!" said Winifred in disgust. "To think

25

you're nearly fifteen and you don't know how to clean boots! How shocking! All the more reason why you should learn at once. Go back to Belinda's study and try to do what she tells you. I know she's hot-tempered and will tick you off properly, but honestly I think you both deserve it. Do have a little common sense."

Winifred turned back to her books. The twins, red in the face, went out of the room and closed the door quietly. They stood outside and looked at each other.

"I shan't clean her beastly boots, even if I have to stay in the school grounds the whole of the term and not go down into the town once," said Pat, angrily.

"Oh, Pat! I do want to get a new set of hair-grips and some chocolate," said Isabel, in dismay. "Come on – we'd better do it. The others will think we're terribly silly if we kick up such a fuss. They laugh at us enough already."

"Well, you can do it if you like, but *I'm* not going to!" said Pat, and she stalked off, her nose in the air, leaving Isabel by herself.

Isabel stood for a little while, thinking. "Supposing I go and do the jobs that Belinda wants done," she thought. "That means that I can go down into the town if I want to – and as Pat is so exactly like me, she can go down too, if we each go at different times, with some-body else. No one will ever know! That will trick Belinda nicely!"

Isabel went to Belinda's study. It was empty. On the floor lay two pairs of very muddy boots. The owners had evidently been across some very clayey fields. Isabel picked them up. Goodness, however did anyone set about cleaning boots like that?

She heard some one passing and went to the door. She saw Kathleen Gregory and called her.

"Kathleen! Look at these awful boots! How do I clean them?"

The Twins marched to Winifred's study

Kathleen stopped at once, looking delighted. She was pleased that Isabel should ask her help. "You want to scrape them first and get all the clay off," she said. "Come on, I'll help you."

Soon the two girls were cleaning the muddy boots thoroughly. They took quite a time. Kathleen talked hard all the time, pouring out all kinds of information about how her mother spoilt her at home, and what a lot of presents she was always getting from her parents, and how much money they sent her for her birthday.

Isabel listened politely, grateful for Kathleen's help, but thinking that she was rather silly. After all, every one got presents for their birthdays, and every one had money on their birthdays! When the boots were finished she put them neatly together on the shoe-shelf, and made up the fire. Kathleen showed her where to fill the kettle and set it on to boil. Just then Belinda and Pam came back.

"Oh, so you decided to be sensible, I see," she said. "Where's your twin? Did she help you?"

"No," said Isabel.

"Well, tell her from me that there's to be no going down to the town till she does her bit," said Belinda, flinging herself down in a chair. "I won't have new girls behaving as if they owned the place! Is the kettle boiling yet? My goodness, the water's cold! How long has this kettle been on?"

"I've only just this minute put it on, Belinda," said Isabel.

"I suppose it didn't occur to you that it would be a good idea to make up the fire and put the kettle on *first*, before you did the boots?" said Belinda, sarcastically. "I suppose you thought it would be a great pity if the kettle boiled whilst you were doing the boots? I don't know what you kids are coming to nowadays. When I was your age I had a lot more common sense. Clear out

28

now. And see that you come running next time I send a message!"

Isabel went out of the room. Just as she was closing the door Belinda yelled to her again. "And mind you tell that obstinate twin of yours what I said. If she disobeys I'll report her to Miss Theobald."

Isabel fled. She felt upset and angry and very foolish. Why, why, why hadn't she put the kettle on first? No wonder that Belinda had thought her stupid.

Isabel told Pat what had happened. "And she says you're not to go down to the town till you do your bit," she said. "But you can, Pat – because no one will know if it's you or me going! I don't think anyone can tell the difference between us yet."

"All right," said Pat, ungraciously. "But I don't think much of you for giving in like that, Isabel. Fancy cleaning those dirty boots!"

"Well, I rather enjoyed it," said Isabel. "Kathleen helped me. First we . . ."

"Oh, shut up," said Pat, rudely. "Go and write an essay about how to clean boots and boil kettles if you want to, but don't preach to me!"

Isabel was hurt. But Pat could not be angry with her twin for long. Before an hour had gone by she had slipped her arm through Isabel's. "Sorry, old thing," she said. "I wasn't really angry with you. I was furious with Belinda, and took it out on you. Never mind! I'll trick Belinda all right and go down to the town whenever I like, pretending that I am you."

Pat was as good as her word! She slipped down to the town with one or other of the girls, pretending that she was Isabel, and nobody knew the difference! How the twins giggled about their trick!

And then something happened. Pat had gone down to the town with Kathleen after tea, when a messenger came to the common-room. Isabel was winding up the gramophone, and she jumped when she heard Pat's name called.

"Patricia O'Sullivan! Belinda wants you!"

"Well – I must pretend to be Pat," thought Isabel. "But why does Belinda want Pat? I'm the one that does her jobs just now. She knows Pat doesn't."

She soon knew what Belinda wanted. The sports-captain was making out a list and she looked up as Isabel came in.

"Pat O'Sullivan, you played well in the lacrosse practice yesterday," she said. "I was watching. You're a silly, obstinate kid, but I'm not counting that against you where lacrosse is concerned. I'm putting you down for the match on Saturday."

Isabel stared in surprise. How pleased Pat would be! Isabel muttered a thank you and sped, longing for Pat to come back so that she might tell her the good news.

When Pat heard she stood speechless. "In a match already!" she cried. "How decent of Belinda! If she'd been spiteful she'd have left me out for months."

Then she became silent and went away by herself. Isabel knew quite well what she was thinking, because she was worrying about the same thing herself.

Soon Pat came over and put her arm through Isabel's. "I feel a beast now," said Pat. "I've let you do all the jobs – and I've gone down to the town all I wanted to, just to spite Belinda. I thought we were being rather clever to play a trick like that. But now I don't think so."

"Nor do I," said Isabel. "I just feel mean and dishonest. It was decent of Belinda to stick you in the match, although she must have felt furious with you – but *we* haven't been decent. And, you know, Pat, I don't really mind doing anything for the top-formers. They are awfully good sorts, really. After all, why should anyone mind putting a kettle on to boil and making toast? Belinda talks to me quite a lot now, and I like

30

her, though I'm a bit afraid of her hot temper."

Pat rubbed her nose and frowned. She always did that when she felt uncomfortable. She suddenly got up and went to the door. "I'm going to tell Belinda I've played her a trick," she said. "I'm not playing in the match on Saturday knowing I've been mean."

She ran out. She went to Belinda's study and knocked on the door. Belinda yelled, "Come in!" She looked surprised when she saw Pat.

"Hallo, Isabel!" she said. "I didn't send for you."

"I'm not Isabel, I'm Pat," said Pat. "I've come about the match on Saturday."

"Well, there's nothing more to tell you than I told you just now," said Belinda.

"That's just it. You didn't tell *me* just now – you told my twin, Isabel," said Pat. "I was down in the town. I know you said I wasn't to go – but I'm so like my twin that I knew nobody would ever know."

"Rather a mean trick, Pat," said Belinda, in a scornful voice.

"I know," said Pat, in a troubled voice. "I'm sorry for that. I've come to say thank you for putting me in the match, but of course I don't expect to play now. Anyway, I couldn't have you being decent to me if I was playing a trick just to pay you out. And I'll take my share of the jobs with Isabel now. I was silly before. That's all, Belinda."

"No – not quite all," said Belinda, in an unexpectedly gentle voice. "I've something to say too. You've done something rather mean, but you've been big enough to put it right. We'll say no more about it – but you'll play in the match on Saturday!"

Pat flew off to tell Isabel, her heart leaping for joy. How decent Belinda was! How could she ever have thought her beastly and horrid?

"I'll boil her old kettle and clean her old boots and even scrub the floor now!" thought Pat. "And my word I'll shoot a dozen goals on Saturday, see if I don't!"

She didn't – but she shot one very difficult one – and how pleased she was to hear both Isabel *and* Belinda shout, "Well done, Pat! Oh, good shot, good shot!"

A Battle With Mam'zelle

Every week the twin's form had marks for different subjects. Pat and Isabel had been used to being top in most things at Redroofs, and it was with shame and dismay that they found they were nearer the bottom than the top at St. Clare's.

Hilary saw them looking unhappy about it and she spoke to them. "You've got to remember that you are the only new girls in your form," she said. "The rest of us have been in the form at least two terms, and we are used to St. Clare ways. Cheer up!"

It was "Mam'zelle Abominable" who really upset the twins. She would not make allowances for them, and when they sent in badly written French essays, she was very angry.

She had the pile of French books on the desk before her, all neatly marked with *"Très bien"* or *"Bien"* or *"Excellent"*. But when she took out Pat's book and Isabel's they were both marked the same. "Abominable!"

"This will not do!" cried Mam'zelle, banging her big hand down on the books. *"C'est abominable!* You will write the whole essay again today, and you will bring it to me after supper."

"We can't write it again today, Mam'zelle," said Isabel, politely. "We've got art this afternoon, and after tea we've got permission to go to the cinema together. We shan't have time to rewrite it. Can we do it tomorrow?"

"Oh, *que vous êtes* insupportable!" raged Mam'zelle, stamping her foot on the floor, and making the books on her desk jump and slide. "How dare you talk to me like this! You present me with a shocking, yes, a shocking essay, and then you talk of going to the cinema. You will not go! You will stay behind and write the essay for me. And if there is more than one mistake you will write it all over again! That is certain!"

"But – but – we've got the tickets," said Isabel. "We had to book our seats. We . . ."

"I do not care about seats, I do not care about booking!" shouted Mam'zelle, now quite losing her temper. "All I care about is that you should learn good French, which is what I am here for. You will bring me the essays tonight."

Isabel looked ready to cry. Pat looked mutinous, and stuck out her lower lip. Every one else enjoyed the row and a few of the girls were secretly very pleased to see the twins taken down a peg. Nobody dared to be inattentive after that, and the lesson went very smoothly, though Pat was sulky and joined in the lesson as little as she dared.

When the lesson was over the twins had a few words together. I'm going to the cinema!" said Pat.

"Oh, no, Pat!" said Isabel, shocked. "We can't do that. We'd really get into a terrible row. We'd better stay behind and do the work again. For goodness' sake let's!"

"I'm GOING to the cinema!" said Pat, obstinately. "I'll fit in the beastly essay somehow, and you must too. Let's do it directly after dinner. I don't care how badly I do it either."

But after dinner they had to go to a meeting of their

form to plan nature rambles, so there was no time then. Art took up the whole of the afternoon. Isabel began to be worried. Suppose Pat insisted on going to the cinema even if they hadn't rewritten their essays? She could not imagine what Mam'zelle would say.

"Let's miss our tea," said Isabel to Pat as they ran down the stairs after the art lesson. "We could do our essays then."

"Miss my tea! No, thank you!" said Pat. "I'm jolly hungry. I don't know why art makes me hungry, but it always does. And I know Janet has got a big pot of plum jam sent to her that she's opening this tea time. I'm not going to miss my share!"

Isabel was hungry too, and she weakly gave way. She knew that if they were going to get into the cinema in time they wouldn't have a moment to spare for anything after tea, let alone rewriting essays! "I really shan't go to the cinema," she thought. "I daren't. Honestly, I think Mam'zelle Abominable would go up in smoke if she heard we'd gone."

But after tea Pat dragged Isabel off to the dormitory to get her hat and coat. "We're not really going, Pat, surely!" cried Isabel.

"Indeed we are!" said Pat, sticking out her lower lip. "Come on."

"But, Pat – we'll really get into a simply enormous row!" said Isabel. "It isn't worth it. Perhaps Mam'zelle will give us an hour's extra work every day or something like that. Janet told me that once she had to stop in after tea for a whole week and write out French verbs for cheeking Mam'zelle just a little bit. And she wouldn't count this a little thing."

"Don't be a coward, Isabel," said Pat. "I've got a plan. Mam'zelle said we were to take our essays to her after supper, didn't she? But she didn't say what time after supper! So when we're in bed and think the others

34

are asleep, we'll slip down to the common room in our dressing-gowns, rewrite our essays then – and give them to Mam'zelle when they're finished!"

"Pat! I'd never dare to!" cried poor Isabel. "Think of going to find Mam'zelle at that time of night in our dressing-gowns. You must be mad."

"Well, Mam'zelle has *made* me feel mad," said obstinate Pat. "Anyway, I don't care what happens. You know we never wanted to come to St. Clare's – and if it's going to treat us like this, I'm jolly sure I won't stay. I'll get expelled!"

"Pat, you're not to say things like that!" said Isabel. "Think what Mummy and Daddy would say!"

"Well it's their fault for sending us here," said Pat, who really was in a great rage.

"Yes, but, Pat – think how awful it would be if Redroofs heard that we'd been sent away from St. Clare's," said Isabel, in a low voice.

Pat's eyes filled with tears. She didn't want to think of that. "Come on," she said, gruffly. "I'm not going to change my mind now. If you're coming with me, come. If not, you can jolly well be a coward by yourself!"

But Isabel was not going to be left by herself. She put on her hat and coat. Janet came into the room as the twins were going out.

"Hallo, hallo!" she said. "So you *are* going to the cinema after all! Whenever did you find time to rewrite your French?"

"We haven't done it," said Pat. Janet gave a long whistle and stared at the twins in surprise.

"I wouldn't like to be in your shoes tomorrow when you tell Mam'zelle that!" she said. "You really are a couple of idiots. I can't think why you should go out of your way to make things difficult for yourselves!"

The twins did not answer. They ran downstairs and were soon in the town. But neither of them really enjoyed the show, although it was a fine nature-film. They had to leave a little before the end to get back to supper in time. There was a debate afterwards that they had to go to, and they both wished they could miss it. But it was taken by Winifred James, the head-girl, and neither of the twins dared to ask if they might miss it.

Nine o'clock was the bedtime for their form and the two forms above them. Chattering and laughing, the girls went upstairs and undressed. Usually a mistress came to see that all the girls were in bed, and switched off the lights – but tonight Hilary announced that she was to see to this.

"Miss Roberts is with Miss Theobald," she said, "so I'm on duty tonight. Hurry, all of you, because the light will go off in five minutes' time, and you'll have to finish in the dark if you're not ready."

Two girls, Joan and Doris, began to have a pillow-fight when they heard that Miss Roberts was not coming. Bang-thud went the two pillows, and the girls shrieked with laughter. But it wasn't quite so funny when one of the pillows split and feathers poured out into the air!

"Golly!" said Joan. "Look at my pillow. Hilary, for goodness' sake don't turn the lights off yet. I *must* pick up some of these feathers!"

"Sorry," said Hilary. "You'll have to do it in the morning. Lights are going out now! Miss Roberts will be along to see we're all right in an hour's time, so let's hope she won't spot the feathers all over the place. She'll think the cat's been chasing hens in our dormitory!"

The lights snapped out. All the girls were in bed except Joan and Doris, who were still groping for feathers. They had to finish undressing and cleaning their teeth in the dark. Joan upset her tooth-mug and Doris banged her ankle on her chest-of-drawers and groaned deeply. Janet giggled, and Kathleen Gregory went off into a

36

spasm of laughter that gave her hiccups.

"Shut up, Kathleen," ordered Hilary. "You're hiccupping on purpose. I know you!"

"I'm *not*!" said Kathleen, indignantly, and gave such an enormous hiccup that her bed shook. Janet couldn't stop giggling. Every time she tried to stop, poor Kathleen hiccupped again and Janet went off into more gurgles.

Even the twins, anxious though they were to have every one going to sleep quickly, could not help laughing. Hilary lost her temper and sat up in bed.

"You're all meanies!" she cried. "If any one comes along and hears you making this row I'll be blamed because I'm head of the dormitory. Shut up, Janet – and Kathleen, for goodness' sake get a drink of water. How do you suppose we're going to sleep with you hiccupping like that?"

"Sorry, Hilary," said Kathleen, with another hiccup. "I'll get up and get some water."

"Get into bed, Joan and Doris," said Hilary, snuggling down again. "I don't care if you've cleaned your teeth and brushed your hair or not. GET INTO BED!"

In five minutes' time there was peace in the dormitory except for an occasional small and subdued hiccup from Kathleen and a smothered giggle from Janet.

The twins lay awake, listening for the others to go to sleep. They were worried because Miss Roberts was coming in about an hour's time. They could not wait a whole hour before going down to the common room. For one thing, Mam'zelle would have gone to bed by the time they had finished their essays!

"Isabel!" whispered Pat at last. "Isabel! I think they're all asleep. Get up and put on your dressing-gown."

"But Miss Roberts hasn't been in yet," whispered back Isabel.

"We'll put our bolsters down our beds, so that they'll look like our bodies," said Pat. "Come on!"

They got up quietly and slipped on their dressing-gowns. They pushed their bolsters down their beds and hoped that Miss Roberts wouldn't notice anything different when she came. Then out of the door they went, and down the dimly-lit stairs to the common room, which was just below their own dormitory.

Pat shut the door and turned on the light. The two girls sat down and took out their French books. Mam'-zelle had marked all the mistakes, and carefully and laboriously the two girls wrote out the essays again.

"Well, mine had fifteen mistakes before, and I hope it hasn't got more than five now!" said Isabel. "Blow Mam'zelle Abominable! I'm so sleepy. And oh, Pat – *dare* we go and find Mam'zelle now, do you think? My knees are shaking at the very thought!"

"Oh, don't be stupid," said Pat. "What can she say to us, anyway? We've done the essays again – and she said give them to her after supper – and we are going to do that, aren't we?"

The essays were finished. Now they had to find Mam'-zelle. Where would she be? In one of the mistresses' common rooms – or in her own bedroom – or where?

"Well, come on," said Pat, at last. "We must go and find her. Cheer up, Isabel."

The twins slipped out of the common room and went to the first of the mistresses' rooms. The light was out and the room was quite dark. No one was there at all. As they went on their way to the second common room, they heard Mam'zelle's voice in one of the classrooms! What luck!

"She's in the upper third classroom," whispered Pat. "I don't know who's there with her, but it doesn't matter. The art mistress, I expect – Mam'zelle's awfully friendly with Miss Walker."

They knocked at the upper third door. A surprised voice called "Come in! Who's there?"

Pat opened the door and the twins went in. And oh my goodness, who should be with Mam'zelle, studying a big French chart, but the Head, Miss Theobald herself!

The twins were so shocked that they stood and stared with wide eyes. Mam'zelle cried *"Tiens!"* in a loud and amazed voice, and Miss Theobald said nothing at all.

Mam'zelle recovered first. "What is wrong?" she cried. "Are you ill, *mes petites*?"

"No," said Pat, in rather a trembling voice. "We're not ill. We've brought you our re-written essays. You said we were to bring them after supper, so here they are."

"But why bring them so late?" asked Miss Theobald, in her deep, serious voice. "You must have known that Mam'zelle meant you to bring them before you went to bed."

"We hadn't time to rewrite the essays till just now," answered Pat, suddenly feeling very foolish indeed. "We got out of bed and went down to the common room to do them."

"Ah! The bad children! They went to the cinema after all, instead of doing my essays!" cried Mam'zelle, guessing everything at once. "Ah, Miss Theobald, these twins send my hair grey! The work they do! It is impossible that they have gone to a school before they came here! Their work is abominable."

"We *did* go to a school, and it was a jolly fine one!" cried Pat, indignantly. *"Much* better than St. Clares!"

There was a silence after this. Miss Theobald looked thoughtful. Mam'zelle was speechless.

"I think we won't decide anything tonight or talk about this," said Miss Theobald at last. "It is too late. Go to bed, twins, and come and see me at ten o'clock tomorrow morning. Ask Miss Roberts to excuse you for fifteen minutes then."

So back to bed with their French books went the twins, subdued and dismayed. What bad luck to have run into the Head herself like that! Now what was going to happen to them? They didn't like to think of ten o'clock in the morning!

Poor Miss Kennedy!

Hilary was awake when they got back into bed and she sat up and demanded to know where they had been.

"Miss Roberts came in and turned on the light and I woke up," said Hilary. "I spotted that you'd put bolsters down your beds, but Miss Roberts didn't. Whatever have you been doing?"

Pat told her. Hilary listened in amazement. "Whatever will you two do next?" she said. "Honestly, I think you're mad. Nobody would ever think you'd been head-girls in your old school. You behave like a couple of babies!"

The twins were annoyed with Hilary, particularly as they each had a kind of feeling that she was right. They got into bed and lay thinking. It was all very well to be defiant and daring – but it wasn't so funny afterwards!

They asked Miss Roberts to excuse them at ten o'clock. Miss Roberts had evidently been told to expect this, for she nodded her head at once, and did not ask any questions. The twins went off together to Miss Theobald's room.

The head was making out time-tables and she told them to sit down for a minute. It was rather dreadful waiting for her to finish what she was doing. Both the twins felt much more nervous than they pretended. Pat began to wonder if the Head would write home about them to their parents. Much as she had grumbled about going to St. Clare's, she didn't want the Head to report her for misbehaviour at the school.

At last Miss Theobald was ready. She swung her chair round and faced the twins. She looked very serious, but not angry.

"I have been looking through the reports that your father sent me from your last school," the Head began. "They are very good, and you seem to have been responsible and conscientious children there. I can't imagine that you can have completely changed your characters in a few weeks, so I am not going to treat you as naughty irresponsible girls. I know there must be a good reason behind all your queer behaviour last night. Really, my dears, you gave Mam'zelle and me quite a shock when you walked into the classroom in your blue dressing-gowns."

The Head smiled. The twins felt most relieved, and Pat began to pour out what had happened in the French class.

"The French isn't the same as at our old school. It isn't much use our trying to do well, because we always get everything wrong. It isn't our fault. And Mam'zelle was simply furious with us yesterday, and . . ."

Miss Theobald heard Pat patiently to the end.

"Well, your French difficulties can easily be put right," said the Head Mistress. "I have spoken to Mam'-zelle, and she says that you speak well and understand well, but that you have not been well grounded in the writing of French. She has offered to give you half an hour's extra French a day until you have caught up the others. This is very kind of her because she is extremely busy. All this bother has come from the fact that you were behind your class in one thing – and if you are wil-

41

ling to help to put it right by working hard with Mam'-zelle, there is no need to say any more about your rather silly behaviour last night."

The twins stared at Miss Theobald with mixed feelings. They were most relieved that nothing more was to be said – but oh dear, oh dear – extra French each day! How tiresome! And yet how decent of Mam'zelle Abominable to be willing to help them.

"Thank you, Miss Theobald," said Pat at last. "We'll try. Once we catch up the others, we shan't feel so angry and ashamed when we are scolded in front of the class."

"Well, you won't be scolded if Mam'zelle really feels you are trying," said Miss Theobald. "Now go to her and arrange what time will be best each day for the extra lesson. And don't go marching through the corridors in your dressing-gowns at half-past ten any more!"

"No, Miss Theobald," said the twins, smiling at the Head. Things seemed suddenly brighter. What they had done didn't any longer seem a dreadful piece of misbehaviour likely to be punished in dire ways – but just a silly bit of nonsense that they were both heartily ashamed of. They went out of the room, and skipped down the passage to the common room. Mam'zelle was there, correcting piles of French essays, and muttering to herself as she ticked the pages.

"*Très bien, ma petite* Hilary! Ah, this dreadful girl. Joan! Ah . . . come in!"

The twins went into the mistresses' common room. Mam'zelle beamed at them, and patted them on the shoulder. Although she had an extremely quick and hot temper, she was very good hearted and kind.

"Ah, now we will see how clever you can be at catching up the others," she said. "Every day you will work with me, and we shall be good friends, *n'est ce pas?*"

"Thank you, Mam'zelle," said Pat. "We were rather idiots yesterday. We won't be again!"

"And thank you for saying you'll help us each day," said Isabel.

So that was that, and the classes with Mam'zelle went much more smoothly. Mam'zelle was patient with the twins, and they tried hard.

But nobody tried hard with poor Miss Kennedy! Janet was a born tease and leg-puller, and she gave the unfortunate history-teacher a terrible time. Janet had a wonderful collection of trick-pencils, all of which she tried on Miss Kennedy with enormous success.

One pencil had a point that was made of rubber, so that it wobbled to one side when Miss Kennedy took it to write with. Another pencil had a point that slipped right inside the pencil as soon as any one wrote with it. The girls all watched with intense eagerness as the unfortunate mistress unwarily used these pencils, and gazed at them in surprise when they behaved so queerly.

Then Janet produced a pencil that wouldn't write at all, although it appeared to have a most marvellous point. To see poor Miss Kennedy pressing hard with the pencil, trying her best to write "Very good" with it, sent the whole class into fits of giggles.

"Girls, girls! Please make less noise!" Miss Kennedy said. "Turn to page eighty-seven of your history books. Today I want to tell you how the people lived in the seventeenth century."

The class at once began to turn over the pages of their history books in a most feverish manner, making a noise like the whispering of trees in the wind. They went on and on turning over the pages, muttering "eighty-seven, eighty-seven" to themselves all the time.

"What number did you say, Miss Kennedy?" asked Kathleen, innocently, though she knew very well indeed.

"I said page eighty-seven," said Miss Kennedy, politely. She was always polite, never rude like Mam'-

43

zelle, or sarcastic like Miss Roberts.

"Oh, eighty-seven!" said all the girls at once, and immediately began to turn over their pages the other way, very busy and very serious – until Janet let out a giggle, and then the whole class roared. Miss Kennedy rapped on the desk.

"Please, please," she said, "I do beg you to be quiet and let us get on with the lesson."

"Please, Miss Kennedy, did the people wear clothes in the seventeenth century, or just skins?" asked Janet, in an innocent voice. Miss Kennedy looked surprised.

"Surely you know that they wore clothes," she said. "I have a picture here of the kind of clothes they wore. You should know that they didn't wear skins then, Janet."

"Not even their *own* skins?" asked Janet. This wasn't really at all funny, but the class was now in a state to giggle at anything, and the twins and every one else joined in the laughter.

"Perhaps they had jumped *out* of their skins and that's why they didn't wear any," said Hilary. More giggles followed this, though half the class didn't even catch what Hilary had said.

"Girls, I can't have this, I really can't," said Miss Kennedy. "I shall have to report you."

"Oh, please, please, PLEASE, Miss Kennedy!" chanted the class in a chorus, and one or two girls pretended to sob.

Poor Miss Kennedy! She had to deal with this sort of thing every time, though the upper forms were better behaved. The lower forms did not mean to be cruel or unkind, but they loved a joke and did not stop to think about Miss Kennedy and what she must be feeling. They just thought she was silly and asked for trouble.

One morning, when the class was especially riotous, Janet caught every one's eye. Kathleen giggled, for she

44

knew what had been planned. When Janet gave the signal every girl was to drop her history text book flat on the floor! Janet nodded, and each girl let go her book.

Crash! Miss Kennedy jumped in fright – and the next minute the door opened and in came Miss Roberts! She had been taking a class in the next room, and when the crash of twenty history books had sounded, like a gunshot, she had decided it was time to investigate.

"Miss Kennedy, I don't know if there are any girls' names you would like to report to me," said Miss Roberts, in a very cold voice, "but I shall be glad to have them after morning school. I am sure you find it as difficult as I do to teach with all this noise going on."

Miss Roberts glared at the form, and they sat silent, half the girls going red. Miss Kennedy went red too.

"I'm so sorry for the noise, Miss Roberts," she said. "You see . . ."

But Miss Roberts was gone, shutting the door after her very firmly indeed.

"Kenny won't report any one," whispered Janet to Isabel. "If she did, she'd have to report the whole class, and she would be ashamed to do that."

Miss Kennedy reported no one – but in the secrecy of her bedroom that night she worried and tossed all night long. She had come to St. Clare's because her friend, Miss Lewis, who thought so much of her, was ill – and now Miss Kennedy felt that she was letting her down because the girls were quite out of hand, and she was sure that not one of them had learnt any history worth mentioning that term! And Miss Roberts had come in like that and been so cold and horrid – and had hardly spoken to her in the common room afterwards. Suppose she complained about her to Miss Theobald? It was dreadful to feel herself a failure, and poor Miss

Kennedy did not see how she could possibly turn her failure into anything like success.

"I'm afraid of the girls, that's why!" she said to herself. "And I do hate reporting them, because if I do they will hate me, and then my classes will be worse than ever."

And in the dormitory Janet was planning other tricks to play on poor unsuspecting Miss Kennedy! Janet had brothers, monkeys all of them, and they sent her all kinds of tricks which they themselves tried out in their own classes.

"Pat! Isabel! Are you asleep?" whispered Janet. "I say! My brothers are sending me some fire-cracks! Have you ever heard of them?"

"Never," said the twins. "Whatever are they?"

"Well, you throw them on the fire and they crack and spit and hiss," whispered Janet, in glee. "My seat is next to the fire – so watch out for some fun next week! I expect the parcel will come tomorrow."

The twins giggled. Whatever would Kenny say when the fire began to spit and hiss and crack? They hugged themselves and pictured Miss Kennedy's alarmed expression.

"Janet!" whispered Pat. "Let's . . ."

But Hilary, head of the dormitory, put an end to the whispering. "Shut up!" she said. "You know the rules, don't you? For goodness' sake, go to sleep!"

Janet is up to Tricks

The parcel of "fire-cracks" duly arrived for Janet. She giggled when she took it from the post-rack, and winked at the twins.

46

"I'll undo it in the dormitory after breakfast," she said. "Say you've forgotten something and get permission to go up before prayers."

So Janet and the twins scurried up stairs to the dormitory immediately after breakfast, and for five minutes they gloated over the contents of the parcel. There was a box inside, and this contained about fifty squib-like crackers small and innocent-looking, coloured red and yellow.

"But will they really make much noise?" asked Pat, taking one up. "I shouldn't think they'd do much more than make a gentle pop."

"Don't worry! I'll throw about a dozen on at a time!" said Janet. "There'll be quite an explosion, I promise you. Golly! We'll have some sport!"

With many giggles the girls hurried downstairs as the bell for prayers went. They could hardly wait for the history-lesson to come. It came after the mid-morning break. Janet told some of the other girls what she was going to do, and the whole form was in a great state of expectation. Even Miss Roberts felt there was something up, though the class tried to work well.

At the end of the maths. lesson, just before break, Miss Roberts spoke a few dry words to her form.

"After break you will have your history lesson as usual. I expect you to work as well for Miss Kennedy as you do for me. If you don't, I shall have something serious to say to you all. There is to be no disturbance at all this morning. DO YOU HEAR ME, JANET?"

Janet jumped. She couldn't imagine why Miss Roberts had suddenly picked her out. She did not know that she had been looking extremely guilty!

"Yes, Miss Roberts," said Janet, thinking that, alas, she would not be able to play her fire-crack trick after all.

But the rest of the form crowded round her during

47

break, and insisted that she carried out her promise. They couldn't bear not to have the treat of seeing Miss Kennedy jump and stare with wide eyes at the fire's extraordinary behaviour.

"All right," said Janet, at last. "But for goodness' sake don't give me away to Miss Roberts, that's all, if she hears anything. And DO promise not to laugh too loudly. Honestly, we'll get into an awful row if Miss Roberts hears us. And she'll be quite near, you know."

"No, she won't," said Kathleen. "She's taking the sixth for something. I heard her say so. And they're right at the other end of the school! She won't hear a thing."

"Good," said Janet, feeling more comfortable. "Well, watch out! We'll hear some fine spitting and hissing, I can tell you!"

The whole form were in their places as quiet as mice when Miss Kennedy came in to give them their usual history lesson. She was feeling even more nervous than usual, for she had not forgotten how the form had behaved the last time she had taken them. She was most relieved to see them sitting so quietly in their places.

"Good morning, girls," said Miss Kennedy, sitting at her desk.

"Good morning, Miss Kennedy," chorused the form, and the lesson opened. Miss Kennedy had to turn to the blackboard to draw a history chart, and immediately every girl turned her head towards Janet. The time had come!

Janet's seat was just by the fire. The box of fire-cracks was in her desk. Cautiously she lifted the lid, and took out about a dozen. She threw them into the heart of the fire.

Every one waited tensely. For a moment nothing happened at all except that the fire flamed up a little. Then the excitement began!

Crack! Spit! Hiss! Half the fire-cracks went off at once, and sparks jumped up the chimney and leapt out of the fire on to the floor.

CRACK! Sssssssssss! Every one watched and listened, their eyes on poor Miss Kennedy, who looked as surprised and as startled as could be!

"Miss Kennedy! Oh Miss Kennedy! What's happening!" cried Pat, pretending to be frightened.

"It's all right, Pat – it's probably a very gassy piece of coal," said Miss Kennedy. "It's all over now – but it really made me jump."

"CRACK! CRACK!" some more fireworks went off, and a shower of sparks flew out of the fire. Janet jumped up, took the blackboard-cleaner, and began to beat out the sparks with an enormous amount of quite unnecessary noise.

"Janet! Janet! Stop!" cried Miss Kennedy, afraid that the next class would hear the noise.

By this time the class had begun to giggle, though they had tried hard to keep serious and to smother their laughter. When the fire-cracks went off once more the class nearly went into hysterics, which were not made any better by the sight of Janet again pretending to beat out sparks on the floor by flapping about with the blackboard-cleaner, making an enormous dust.

Miss Kennedy went pale. She guessed that some trick had been played, though she couldn't imagine what. She stood up, looking unexpectedly dignified, though bits of straight hair fell rather wildly from the two knots at the sides of her head.

"Girls!" she said. "There will be no history lesson this morning. I refuse to teach an unruly class like this."

She went out of the room, her face white and her eyes swimming with tears.

She would have to go to the Head and give up her job. She couldn't possibly take fees for teaching girls who simply played the whole of the time. But it was no use going when she felt so upset. She would wait until the end of the morning and go then. She hurriedly scribbled a note to Miss Roberts, and sent it to her by one of the school maids.

"Am afraid I feel unwell, and have had to leave your form for a while," said the note.

Miss Roberts was surprised to get the note. She debated with herself whether to let the first form carry on by itself – surely Miss Kennedy would have left them some work to do? Or should she leave the sixth form to get on by themselves, and go back to the first? She decided to give the sixth some questions to answer, and leave them. They would behave themselves, of course – but she wasn't so sure about her own form!

So she began to write out questions on the board, wondering meanwhile what the first form was up to.

They had been rather taken aback when Miss Kennedy walked out. Some of the girls felt guilty and uncomfortable, but when the fire began to hiss and spit again, it all seemed terribly funny once more, and Doris, Joan, Kathleen and the rest began to giggle again.

"*Did* you see old Kenny when the first crack went off?" cried Joan. "I thought I should die, trying not to laugh. I had an awful stitch in my side, I can tell you."

"Janet, those fire-cracks are simply marvellous!" cried Hilary. "Put some more on – Kenny won't be back. All I hope is that she doesn't go and tell Miss Theobald."

"She didn't go towards the Head's room," said Janet. "She went the other way. All right – I'll stick some more on. Watch out, every one!"

Janet shook the box over the fire, meaning to throw out about a dozen of the little squibs – but the whole lot went in! Janet laughed.

"Golly! They've all gone in. We'll have some fun!"

Doris was at the door of the classroom, keeping guard in case a teacher came along. Suddenly she gave a cry.

"Look out! Miss Roberts is coming! Get to your seats, quick!"

Every one scurried to their seats at once. They pulled open their history books, and by the time that Miss Roberts came into the room, the class looked fairly peaceful, though it was rather surprising to see so many bent heads. Miss Roberts became suspicious at once — usually the girls all looked up when she came into the room!

"You seem very busy," she said, drily. "Did Miss Kennedy leave you history work to do?"

Nobody answered. Janet gave an anxious glance at the fire. Those fire-cracks! How she wished she hadn't put so many on! The fire began to flare up a little. Miss Roberts spoke sharply.

"Can't somebody answer me? Did Miss . . ."

But she did not finish her question, because about twenty fire-cracks went off at once with the most tremendous hissing, spluttering and cracking! Sparks flew out and huge flames shot up the chimney.

"Good heavens!" said Miss Roberts. "What in the world is going on there?"

Again nobody said a word. There was no giggling or laughing this time, no smothered gurgles. Everyone looked scared.

Crack! Sssssss! Crack! Some of the fireworks shot themselves up the chimney and exploded there, bringing down showers of soot. It was hot soot, and flew out over the room. Janet and the girls nearest the fire began to cough and choke.

Come away from the fire, Janet," ordered Miss Roberts. "Those sparks will set fire to your tunic."

The soot flew out again, and black specks began to descend on to books, papers, desks and heads. Miss

51

Roberts' mouth went very straight and thin. She looked round the class.

"Some one has been putting fireworks into the fire," she said. "The class will dismiss. I am going to the common room across the passage. I expect the girl who played this stupid and dangerous joke to come and own up at once."

She left the room. Every one stared in dismay. It was all very well to play a joke on stupid old Kenny – but Miss Roberts was a different matter altogether! Miss Roberts knew a great many most annoying punishments.

"Gosh! I'm in for it now!" said Janet, gloomily. "I'd better go and get it over."

She went to the door. The twins stared after her. Pat ran to the door too.

"Janet! Wait! I'm coming too. I was as much to blame as you, because I egged you on. I'd have put those fire-cracks on if you hadn't!"

"And I'll come as well," said Isabel at once.

"Oh, I say! That *is* decent of you!" said Janet, slipping her arm through Pat's, and holding out her other hand to Isabel.

Then Hilary spoke up too. "Well, I'll come along as well. As a matter of fact, we're all to blame. It's true you got the squibs and put them on – but we all shared the joke, and it's not fair that only you should be punished."

So it ended in the whole of the class going to the common room, looking very downcast and ashamed. Miss Roberts looked up, surprised to see so many girls crowding into the room.

"What's all this for?" she asked, sternly.

"Miss Roberts, may I tell you?" said Hilary. "I'm head of the form."

"I want the person who played the trick to own up," said Miss Roberts. "Who did it?"

"I did," said poor Janet, going rather white. Her knees

shook a little, and she looked on the floor. She could not bear to meet Miss Roberts' sharp hazel eyes.

"But we were all in it," said Hilary. "We wanted Janet to do it, and we shared in it."

"And may I ask if you also treated Miss Kennedy to the same silly trick?" asked Miss Roberts, in her most sarcastic voice.

"Yes," said Janet, in a low voice.

"So that explains it," said Miss Roberts, thinking of the note that Miss Kennedy had sent her. "Well, you will all share the expenses of the chimney being swept and you will all spend two hours each washing down the walls and scrubbing the floor and desks after the sweep has been. That means that you will work in batches of five, each giving up two hours of your free time to do it."

"Yes, Miss Roberts," said the class dolefully.

"You will also apologize to Miss Kennedy, of course," went on Miss Roberts. "And I should like to say that I am ashamed of you for taking advantage of somebody not able to deal with you as I can!"

The form trooped out. Miss Roberts telephoned for the sweep – and Miss Kennedy was surprised to find relays of girls waylaying her, offering her humble apologies for their behaviour. They did not tell her what had happened, so Miss Kennedy had no idea that Miss Roberts had experienced the same startling explosions from the fire, but had dealt with the whole matter with a firm hand. She really thought that the girls were offering their apologies of their own accord, and she felt almost happy.

"I shan't give in my resignation to Miss Theobald after all," she thought. "Anyway, if I did, I would have to say why, and I shouldn't like to give the girls away after they had said they were sorry in such a nice way."

So the matter rested there for a while – and batches of dismal girls washed and scrubbed that afternoon and evening, instead of playing lacrosse, and going to a concert!

One good thing came out of the row – and that was that the twins' form liked them a great deal better.

"It was decent of Pat and Isabel to go after Janet like that and say they'd share the blame," said Hilary. "Good for them!"

The Great Midnight Feast

Miss Roberts kept a very tight hand indeed on her form for the next week or two, and they squirmed under her dry tongue. Pat and Isabel hated being spoken to as if they were nobodies, but they did not dare to grumble.

"It's simply awful being ticked off as if we were in the kindergarten, when we've been used to bossing the whole school at Redroofs," said Isabel. "I shall never get used to it!"

"I hate it too," said Pat. But all the same, I can't help liking Miss Roberts, you know. I do respect her awfully, and you can't help liking people you respect."

"Well, I wish she'd start respecting *us*, then," said Isabel gloomily, "Then maybe she'd like us, and we wouldn't get such a hot time in class. Golly, when I forgot to take my maths. book to her this morning you'd have thought she was going to 'phone up the police station and have me sent to prison!"

Pat laughed. "Don't be an idiot," she said. "By the way, don't forget to give half a crown towards buying Miss Theobald something on her birthday. I've given mine in."

"Oh, my!" groaned Isabel. "I hope I've got half a crown! I had to give sixpence towards the sweep, and

I gave a shilling to the housemaid for cleaning my tunic for me in case Matron ticked me off about it – and we had to give sixpence to the Babies' Convalescent Home last week. I'm just about broke!"

She went to her part of the shelf in the common room and took down her purse. It was empty!

"Golly!" said Isabel in dismay. "I'm sure I had two shillings in my purse. Did you borrow it, Pat?"

"No," said Pat. "Or I'd have told you. It must be in your coat-pocket, silly."

But the two shillings were nowhere to be found. Isabel decided she must have lost them, and she had to borrow some money from Pat to give towards buying the Head a present.

Then Janet had a birthday, and every one went down to the town to buy a small present for her – all but Hilary, who discovered, to her dismay, that the ten-shilling note that her Granny had sent her, had disappeared out of her pocket!

"Oh, my, a whole ten shillings!" wailed Hilary. "I was going to buy all sorts of things with it. I really must get some new shoelaces, and my lacrosse stick wants mending. Where in the world has it gone?"

Joan lent Hilary a shilling to buy a present for Janet, and on her birthday Janet was most delighted to find so many gifts. She was very popular, in spite of her bluntness. The finest gift she had was from Kathleen Gregory, who presented her with a gold bar-brooch, with her name inscribed at the back.

"I say! You shouldn't have done that!" said Janet, in amazement. "Why, it must have cost you a mint of money, Kathleen! I really can't accept it. It's too generous a gift."

"But you *must* accept it, because it's got your name inside," said Kathleen. "It's no use to any one else!"

Every one admired the little gold brooch and read the

name inscribed on the back. Kathleen glowed with pleasure at the attention that her gift produced, and when Janet thanked her again, and slipped her arm through hers, she was red with delight.

"It was very generous of Kathleen," said Janet to the twins, as they went to the classroom. "But I can't understand why she went such a splash on me! Usually she's awfully mean with her gifts – either gives nothing at all, or something that costs half a farthing! It isn't as if she likes me such a lot, either. I've gone for her heaps of times because she's such a goof!"

Janet had a marvellous tuck-hamper sent to her for her birthday, and she and Hilary and the twins unpacked it with glee. "All the things I love!" said Janet. "A big chocolate cake! Shortbread biscuits! Sardines in tomato sauce! Nestlé's milk. And look at these peppermint creams! They'll melt in our mouths!"

"Let's have a midnight feast!" said Pat, suddenly. "We once had one at Redroofs, before we were headgirls. I don't know why food tastes so much nicer in the middle of the night than in the daytime, but it does! Oh, Janet – don't you think it would be fun?"

"It might be rather sport," said Janet. "But there's not enough food here for us all. The rest of you will have to bring something as well. Each girl had better bring one thing – a cake – or ginger-beer – or chocolate. When shall we have the feast?"

"Tomorrow night," said Isabel, with a giggle. "Miss Roberts is going to a concert. I heard her say so. She's going to stay the night with a friend and get a train that brings her back in time for prayers."

"Oh, good! Tomorrow's the night then!" said Janet. "Let's tell every one."

So the whole form was told about the Great feast, and every one promised to bring something. Pat bought a jam sponge sandwich. Isabel, who again had to borrow

56

from Pat, bought a bar of chocolate. Joan brought candles, because the girls were not allowed to put on the electric light once it was turned out except for urgent reasons, such as illness.

The most lavish contribution was Kathleen's! She brought a really marvellous cake, with almond icing all over it, and pink and yellow sugar roses on the top. Every one exclaimed over it!

"Golly, Kathleen! Have you come into a fortune or something!" cried Janet. "That cake must have cost you all your pocket-money for the rest of the term! It's marvellous."

"The prettiest cake I've ever seen," said Hilary. "Jolly decent of you, Kathleen."

Kathleen was red with pleasure. She beamed round at every one, and enjoyed the smiles that she and her cake received.

"I wish I could have got something better than my silly little bar of chocolate," said Isabel. "But I even had to borrow from Pat to get that."

"And I can only bring a few biscuits I had left from a tin that Mother sent me a fortnight ago," said Hilary. "I'm quite broke since I lost my ten-shilling note."

"Anyway, we've got heaps of things," said Janet, who was busy hiding everything at the bottom of a cupboard just outside the dormitory. "Golly, I hope Matron doesn't suddenly take it into her head to spring-clean this cupboard! She *would* be surprised to see what's in it. Goodness – who brought this pork-pie? How marvellous!"

The whole form was in a state of excitement that day. It was simply gorgeous to have a secret and not to let any of the other forms know. Hilary knew that the upper third had had a midnight feast already that term, and it had been a great success. She meant to make theirs even more of a success!

Miss Roberts couldn't think why the first-form girls were so restless. As for Mam'zelle, she sensed the underlying excitement at once, and grew excited too.

"Ah, now, *mes petites,* what is the matter with you today!" she cried, when one girl after another made a mistake in the French translation. "What is in your thoughts? You are planning something – is it not so? Tell me what it is."

"Oh, Mam'zelle, whatever makes you think such a thing!" cried Janet. "What should we be planning?"

"How should I know?" said Mam'zelle. "All I know is that you are not paying attention. "Now, one more mistake and I send you to bed an hour earlier than usual!"

Mam'zelle did not mean this, of course – but it tickled the girls, who were all longing for bedtime that night, and would have been quite pleased to go early. Janet giggled and was nearly sent out of the room.

At last bedtime came, and every one undressed.

"Who's going to get the stuff out of the cupboard?" said Pat.

"You and I and Hilary and Isabel," said Janet. "And for goodness' sake don't drop anything. If you drop the pork-pie on the linoleum there *will* be a mess."

Every one laughed. They snuggled down into bed. They all wanted to keep awake, but it was arranged that some of them should take it in turns to sit up and keep awake for half an hour, waking the next girl when it was her turn. Then, at midnight, they should all be awakened and the Feast would begin!

First Janet sat up in bed for half an hour, hugging her knees, and thinking of all the things in the cupboard outside. She was not a bit sleepy. She switched on her torch to look at the time. The half-hour was just up. She leaned across to the next bed and awoke Hilary.

At midnight every one was fast asleep except for the

girl on watch, who was Pat. As she heard the big clock striking from the west tower of the school, Pat crept out of bed. She went from girl to girl, whispering in her ear and shaking her.

"Hilary! It's time! Wake up! Isabel! It's midnight! Joan! The Feast is about to begin. Kathleen! Kathleen! Do wake up! It's twelve o'clock!"

At last every girl was awake, and with many smothered giggles, they put on their dressing-gowns and slippers.

The whole school was in darkness. Pat lighted two candles, and placed them on a dressing-table in the middle of the dormitory. She had sent Isabel to waken the rest of the form in the next dormitory, and with scuffles and chuckles all the girls crept in. They sat on the beds nearest to the candles, and waited whilst Pat and the others went to get the things out of the cupboard.

Pat took her torch and shone it into the cupboard whilst the others took out the things. A tin of sweetened milk dropped to the floor with a crash. Every one jumped and stood stock still. They listened, but there was no sound to be heard – no door opened, no one switched on a light.

"Idiot!" whispered Janet to Isabel. "For goodness' sake don't drop that chocolate cake. Where did that tin roll to? Oh, here it is."

At last all the eatables were safely in the dormitory, and the door was shut softly. The girls looked at everything, and felt terribly hungry.

"Golly! Pork-pie and chocolate cake, sardines and Nestlé's milk, chocolate and peppermint creams, tinned pineapple and ginger-beer!" said Janet. "Talk about a feast! I bet this beats the upper third's feast hollow! Come on – let's begin. I'll cut the cake."

Soon every girl was munching hard and thinking that food had never tasted quite so nice before. Janet took

"Talk about a feast!" said Janet

an opener and opened a ginger-beer bottle. The first one was quite all right and Janet filled two tooth-glasses. But the next ginger-beer bottle fizzed out tremendously and soaked the bed that Janet was sitting on. Everyone giggled. It went off with a real pop, and sounded quite loud in the silence of the night.

"Don't worry! No one will hear that," said Janet. "Here, Pat – open the sardines. I've got some bread and butter somewhere, and we'll make sandwiches."

The bread and butter was unwrapped from its paper. Janet had brought it up from the tea-table! Every girl had taken a piece from the plate at tea-time, and hidden it to give to Janet.

"Look – take a bite of a sardine sandwich, and then a bite of pork-pie, and then a spoonful of Nestlé's milk," said Pat. "It tastes gorgeous."

The chocolate was saved till last. By that time the girls were all unable to eat any more and could only suck the sweets and the chocolate. They sat about and giggled at the silliest jokes.

"Of course, the nicest thing of the whole feast was Kathleen's marvellous cake," said Hilary. "The almond icing was gorgeous."

"Yes – and I had one of the sugar roses," said Joan. "Lovely! However much did you pay for that cake, Kath? It was jolly decent of you."

"Oh, that's nothing," said Kathleen. "I'm most awfully glad you liked it."

She looked very happy. There had not been quite enough cake to go round and Kathleen hadn't even tasted the marvellous cake. But she didn't mind at all. She sat quite happily watching the others feast on it.

Then the girls began to press Doris to do her clown-dance. This was a dance she had learnt during the holidays at some special classes, and it was very funny. Doris was full of humour and could make the others laugh very easily. The clown dance was most ridiculous, because Doris had to keep falling over herself. She accompanied this falling about with many groans and gurgles, which always sent the audience into fits of laughter.

"Well, don't laugh too loudly this time," said Doris, getting up. "You made such a row last time I did it in the common room that Belinda Towers came in and ticked me off for playing the fool."

She began the dance with a solemn face. She fell over the foot of the bed, on purpose of course, and rubbed herself with a groan. The girls began to chuckle, their hands over their mouths.

Doris loved making people laugh. She swayed about, making comical faces, then pretended to catch one leg in another, and fell, clutching at Pat with a deep groan.

With a giggle Pat fell too, and knocked against the dressing-table. The table shook violently, and everything on it slid to the floor! Brushes, combs, photograph frames, tooth-mugs, a ginger-beer bottle – goodness, what a crash!

The girls stared in horror. The noise sounded simply terrific!

"Quick! Clear everything up and get into bed," cried Janet, in a loud whisper. "Golly! We'll have half the mistresses here."

The girls belonging to the next dormitory fled out of the door at once. The others cleared up quickly, but very soon heard the sound of an electric light being switched on in the passage.

"Into bed!" hissed Hilary, and they all leapt under the sheets. They pulled them up to their chins and lay listening. Hilary remembered that they had left two ginger-beer bottles out in the middle of the floor – and they hadn't had time to clear up the remains of the pork-pie either. Pork-pies were so untidy, and *would* scatter themselves in crumbs every time a bite was taken!

The door opened, and some one was outlined against the light from the passage outside. Pat saw who it was – old Kenny! What bad luck! If she discovered anything she would be sure to report it after the bad behaviour of the form. But perhaps she wouldn't switch on the dormitory light.

Miss Kennedy stood listening. One of the girls gave a gentle snore, making believe that she was fast asleep – but that was too much for Kathleen, who was already very strung up. She gave a smothered giggle, and Miss Kennedy heard it. She switched on the light.

The first thing she saw were the two ginger-beer bottles standing boldly in the middle of the floor. Then she saw the remains of the pork-pie. She saw the paper from the chocolate. She guessed immediately what the girls had been up to.

A little smile came over her face. What monkeys girls were! She remembered the thrill of a midnight feast herself – and how she and the others had been caught and severely punished. She spoke in a low voice to Hilary, the head of the dormitory.

"Hilary! Are you awake?"

Hilary dared not pretend. She answered in a sleepy voice. "Hallo, Miss Kennedy! Is anything wrong?"

"I thought I heard a noise from this dormitory," said Miss Kennedy. "I'm in charge of it tonight as Miss Roberts isn't here. But I may have been mistaken."

Hilary sat up in bed and saw the ginger-beer bottles. She glanced at Miss Kennedy and saw a twinkle in her eye.

"Perhaps you *were* mistaken, Miss Kennedy," she said. "Perhaps – perhaps – it was mice or something."

"Perhaps it *was*," said Miss Kennedy. "Er – well, I don't see that there's anything to report to Miss Roberts – but as you're head of the dormitory, Hilary, you might

63

see that it's tidy before Matron goes her rounds to-morrow morning. Good night."

She switched off the light, shut the door and went back to her room. The girls all sat up in bed at once and began to whisper.

"My goodness! Kenny's a sport!'

"Golly! She saw those awful ginger-beer bottles all right! And fancy agreeing that that terrific noise we made might have been *mice*!"

"And she as good as said we were to remove all traces of the feast, and she promised not to report anything to Miss Roberts."

"Though old Roberts is a sport too, in her way," said Doris.

"Yes, but we're in her bad books at the moment, don't forget, and anything like this would just about finish things!" said Isabel. "Good old Kenny!"

A Lacrosse Match – and a Puzzle

The only bad effects of the Great Midnight Feast, as it came to be called, were that Isabel, Doris and Vera didn't feel at all well the next day. Miss Roberts eyed them sharply.

"What have you been eating?" she asked.

"Only what the others have," answered Doris, quite truthfully.

"Well, go to Matron and she'll dose you," said Miss Roberts. The three girls went off dolefully. Matron had some most disgusting medicine. She dosed the girls generously and they groaned when she made them lick the spoon round.

Then Joan and Kathleen felt ill and they were sent to Matron too.

64

"I know these symptoms," said Matron. "You are suffering from Midnight Feast Illness! Aha! You needn't pretend to me! If you *will* feast on pork-pies and sardines, chocolate and ginger-beer in the middle of the night, you can expect a dose of medicine from me the next day."

The girls stared at her in horror. How did she know?

"Who told you?" asked Joan, thinking that Miss Kennedy had told tales after all.

"Nobody," said Matron, putting the cork back firmly into the enormous bottle. "But I haven't been Matron of a girls' school for twenty-five years without knowing a *few* things! I dosed your mother before you, Joan, and your aunt too. They couldn't stand midnight food any more than you can. Go along now – don't stare at me like that. I shan't tell tales – and I always say there's no need to punish girls for having a midnight feast, because the feelings they get the next day are punishment enough!"

The girls went away. Joan looked at Kathleen. "You know, I simply loved the pork-pie and the sardines last night," she said, gloomily, "but the very thought of them makes me feel sick today. I don't believe I'll ever be able to look a sardine in the face again."

But every one soon forgot their aches and pains, and the feast passed into a legend that was told throughout the school. Even Belinda Towers heard about it and chuckled when she was told how everything fell off the dressing-table at the last.

It was Kathleen who told Belinda. It was rather strange how Kathleen had altered during the last few weeks. She was no longer nervous and apologetic to every one, but took her place happily and laughed and joked like the rest. She could even talk to tall Belinda Towers without stammering with nervousness! She was waiting on Belinda that week, and rushed about quite happily, making toast, running errands and not even grumbling when Belinda sent for her in the middle of a concert rehearsal.

Kathleen was to play in an important lacrosse match that week, and so was Isabel. They were the only first-form girls chosen – all the others were second-formers. At first Pat had been by far the better of the two, but Isabel soon learnt the knack of catching and throwing the ball in the easiest way, and had out-stripped her twin. The match was to be against the second form of a nearby day school, and the girls were very keen about it.

"Kathleen's goalkeeper," said Pat to Isabel. "Belinda told her today. I say, isn't Kath different? I quite like her now."

"Yes – and she's so generous!" said Isabel. "She bought some sweets yesterday and shared the whole lot round without having even one herself. And she bought some chrysanthemums for Vera – they must have cost a lot!"

Vera was in the sick-bay, recovering from a bad cold. She had been very surprised and touched when Kathleen had taken her six beautiful yellow chrysanthemums. It was so unlike Kathleen, who had always been rather mean before.

Kathleen got Isabel to practise throwing balls into the goal, so that she might get even better at stopping them. She was very quick. Then she and Isabel pract-ised catching and throwing the ball and running with it and dodging each other.

"If only, only I could shoot two or three goals on Saturday," Isabel said a dozen times a day. Hilary laughed. Isabel asked her why.

"I'm laughing at *you*," said Hilary. "Who turned up her nose at lacrosse a few weeks ago? You did! Who said there wasn't any game worth playing except hockey? You did! Who vowed and declared she would never try to be any good at a silly game like lacrosse? You did. That's why I'm laughing! I have to sit and hear you raving about lacrosse now, talking it all day long. It sounds funny to me."

Isabel laughed too, but she went rather red. "I must have seemed rather an idiot," she said.

"You *were* a bit of a goof," said Janet, joining in. "The stuck-up twins! That's what we used to call you."

"Oh," said Isabel, ashamed. She made up her mind to play so well on Saturday that her whole form would be proud of her. The stuck-up twins! What a dreadful name! She and Pat must really do something to make the form forget that.

Saturday came, a brilliantly fine winter's day. The first form were excited. The girls from the day-school were coming to lunch and they had to entertain them. Dinner was to be sausages and mashed potatoes, with treacle pudding to follow, a very favourite meal.

"Now look here, Isabel and Kathleen, just see you don't eat too much," ordered Hilary. "We want you to play your best. You're the only ones from the first form who are playing – all the rest are second-formers. We'll stuff the other school all right – give them so much to eat that they won't be able to catch a ball!"

"Oh, I say! Can't I have two sausages?" said Isabel in dismay. "And I always have two helpings of treacle pudding."

"Well, you won't today," said Janet, firmly. "But if you play well and we win, the whole form will stand you cream-buns at tea-time. See?"

So Isabel cheered up and went without a second helping of treacle pudding quite amiably. It was a pleasant lunch. The guests were all jolly, friendly girls, and how they laughed when they were told the story of the Great Feast!

"We can't have fun like that," said one of the day-girls. "We always go home at night. What's your lacrosse team like? Any good? We've beaten you each time we've played you so far."

"And I bet we'll beat them again," cried the captain, a tall girl with flaming red hair.

"Cream-buns for you if you stop their goals, Kathleen!" cried Janet, and every one laughed.

All the first, second and third forms turned out to watch the match. The fourth form were playing a match of their own away from home, and the sixth rarely bothered to watch the juniors. Some of the fifth turned up, among them Belinda Towers, who arranged all the matches and the players, for she was sports-captain, and very keen that St. Clare's should win as many matches as possible.

The players took their places. Isabel was tremendously excited. Kathleen was quite cool and calm in goal. The match began.

The day girls made a strong team, and were splendid runners. They got the ball at once, and passed it from one to another whenever they were tackled. But Isabel jumped high into the air and caught the ball as it flew from one day girl to another!

Then she was off like the wind, racing down the field. A girl came out to tackle and tried to knock the ball off Isabel's net – but Isabel jerked it neatly over her head into the waiting net of another St. Clare girl – and she was off down the field too. Isabel sped behind – and caught the ball again neatly as the other girl threw it when tackled.

But a very fast girl was after Isabel and took the ball from her. Back the other way raced the day-girl, making for the goal. She passed the ball to another girl, who passed it to a third – and the third one shot straight at the goal, where Kathleen stood on guard. Swift as lightning Kathleen put her net down towards the ball, caught it and threw it to Isabel who was waiting not far off.

"Jolly well saved, Kathleen!" roared every one of the St. Clare girls, and Kathleen went red with excitement and delight.

So the match went on till half-time, when lemon quarters were taken round on plates to all the hot and panting players. How they loved sucking the cool sour lemon!

"The score is three-one," said the umpire. "Three to the day-girls of St. Christopher's and one to St. Clare's."

"Play up, St. Clare's!" cried Belinda. "Play up. Now, Isabel, score, please!"

The second half of the match began. The players were not quite so fast now, for they were tired. But the excitement ran very high, especially when St. Clare's shot two goals in quick succession, one of them thrown by Isabel.

Kathleen hopped about on one leg as the play went on down the other end of the field. She had saved seven goals already. Down the field raced the players, the ball flying from one to another with grace and ease. Kathleen stood tensely, knowing that a goal would be tried.

The ball came down on her, hard and swift. She tried to save the goal, but the ball shot into the corner of the net. Goal! Four-three – and only five minutes to go!

Then St. Clare's scored a most unexpected goal in the next two minutes and that made the score equal.

"Only one and a half minutes more!" panted Isabel to a St. Clare girl as she passed her the ball. "For goodness' sake, let's get another goal and win!"

The ball came back to her. A day girl thundered down on Isabel, a big, burly girl. Isabel swung round and dodged, the ball still in her net. She passed it to another girl, who neatly passed it back as soon as she was tackled. And then Isabel took a look at the goal, which, although a good way away, was almost straight in front. It was worth a shot!

She threw the ball hard and straight down the field. The goalkeeper stood ready – but somehow she missed the ball and it rolled into the net, just before the whistle went for time! How the St. Clare girls cheered! Pat leapt up and down like a mad thing, Belinda yelled till she was hoarse, and Hilary and Janet thumped one another on the back, though neither of them quite knew why!

"Good old Isabel! She saved the match just in time!" cried Pat. "Cream-buns for her!"

Hot and tired and happy, all the girls trooped off the field to wash and tidy themselves before tea. Janet ran to get her purse to rush off on her bicycle to buy the cream-buns.

But her purse only had a few pence inside! How strange! Janet knew quite well that it had had five shillings in it that very morning – and she certainly hadn't spent any of it.

"I say! My money's gone!" she said in dismay. "I can't get the cream-buns. Dash! Where's it gone?"

"Funny," said Isabel. "Mine went a little while ago – and so did Hilary's. Now yours has gone."

"Well, don't discuss it now," said Joan. "We've got to entertain the day-girls. But it's a pity about the cream-buns."

"*I'll* buy them!" said Kathleen. "I'll give you the money, Janet."

"Oh, no!" said Janet. "We wanted to buy them for you and Isabel because you did so well in the match. We can't let you buy them for yourselves!"

"Please do," said Kathleen, and she took some money from her pocket. "Here you are. Buy buns for every one!"

"Well – it's jolly decent of you," said Janet, taking the money. "Thanks awfully." She sped off on her bicycle whilst the other girls got ready for tea.

"Well played, kids," said Belinda Towers, strolling up. "You stopped some pretty good goals, Kathleen – and you just about saved the match, Isabel, though all the rest did jolly well too."

Every one glowed at the sports-captain's praise. Then they sat down to tea, and soon the big piles of bread and butter and jam, currant buns and chocolate cake disappeared like magic. Janet was back in a few minutes with a large number of delicious-looking cream-buns. The girls greeted them with cheers.

"Thanks, Kathleen! You're a brick, Kathleen!" everyone cried, and Kathleen beamed with delight.

"Well, I *did* enjoy today!" said Isabel to Pat, as they went off to the common room together, after seeing the day-girls off. "Simply marvellous! Every bit of it."

"Not quite every bit," said Pat, rather gravely. "What about Janet's money? Somebody took that, Isabel. And that's pretty beastly. Who in the world could it be?"

"I simply can't imagine," said Isabel.

Neither could anyone else. The girls talked about it together, and wondered who had been near Janet's coat. She had hung it on a peg in the sports pavilion, and most of the first and second form had been in and out. But surely, surely no St. Clare girl could possibly do such a thing!

"It's stealing, just plain stealing," said Hilary. "And it's been going on for some time too, because I know others besides myself and Janet and Isabel have lost money. Belinda lost ten shillings too. She made an awful row about it, but she never found it."

"Could it be one of the maids?" said Joan.

"Shouldn't think so," said Hilary. "They've been here

for years. Well – we must all be careful of our money, that's all, and, if we can't *find* the thief, we'll make it difficult for her to *be* one!"

A Very Muddled Girl

One afternoon Rita George, one of the big girls, sent for Kathleen to give her some instructions about a nature ramble she was getting up. Kathleen was head of the nature club in her form. She asked Pat to finish winding the wool that Isabel was holding for her, and ran off.

"Shan't be long," she said, and disappeared. Pat wound the wool into balls and then threw them into Kathleen's work-basket. She looked at her watch.

"I hope Kath won't be long," she said. "We are due for gym. in five minutes. I'd better go and remind her. Coming, Isabel?"

The twins went out, and made their way to Rita's study, meaning to see if Kathleen was still there. But when they arrived outside they stood still in dismay.

Some one was sobbing and crying inside! Some one was saying, "Oh, please forgive me! Oh, please don't tell anyone! Please, please, don't!"

"Gracious! That's not Kathleen, is it?" said Pat, horrified. "What's happened?"

They did not dare to go in. They waited, hearing more sobs, pitiful, heartbroken sobs, and they heard Rita's rather deep voice, sounding very stern. They could not hear what she said.

Then the door opened and Kathleen came out, her eyes red, and her cheeks tear-stained. She sobbed under her breath, and did not see the twins. She hurried towards the stairs that led to her dormitory.

72

Pat and Isabel stared after her. "She's forgotten about gym.," said Pat. "I don't like to go to her in case she hates any one seeing her cry."

"Oh, let's go and comfort her," said Isabel. "We'll get into a row for being late for gym. – but it's awful to see any one in trouble like that and not see if we can help."

So they ran up the stairs to the dormitory. Kathleen was lying on her bed, her face buried in her pillow, sobbing.

"Kathleen! Whatever's happened?" asked Isabel, putting her hand on Kathleen's shoulder. Kathleen shook it off.

"Go away!" she said. "Go away! Don't come peeping and prying after me."

"We're not," said Pat, gently. "What's the matter? We're your friends, you know."

"You wouldn't be, if I told you what had happened," sobbed Kathleen. "Oh, do go away. I'm going to pack my things and leave St. Clare's! I'm going this very night!"

"Kathleen! Do tell us what's happened!" cried Isabel. "Did Rita tick you off for something? Don't worry about that."

"It's not the ticking off I'm worrying about – it's the thing I did to *get* the ticking off," said Kathleen. She sat up, her eyes swollen and red. "Well, I'll tell you – and you can go and spread it all round the school if you like – and every one can laugh and jeer at me – but I'll not be here!"

She began to cry again. Pat and Isabel were very much upset. Isabel slipped her arm round the sobbing girl. "All right – tell us," she said. "We won't turn on you, I promise."

"Yes, you will, yes you will! What I've done is so dreadful!" sobbed Kathleen. "You won't believe it! I hardly believe it myself. I'm – I'm – I'm a thief!"

"Kathleen! What do you mean?" asked Pat, shocked. Kathleen stared at her defiantly. She wiped her eyes with a hand that shook.

"*I* took all the money that's been missing!" she said. "Every bit of it – even your two shillings, Isabel. I couldn't bear never having any money of my own, and saying no when people wanted subscriptions, and not giving any nice birthday presents to any one, and being thought mean and selfish and ungenerous. I did so want to be generous to everybody, and to make friends. I do so love giving things and making people happy."

The twins stared at Kathleen in surprise and horror. They could hardly believe what she said. She went on, pouring out her troubles between her sobs.

"I haven't a mother to send me money as you and the other girls have. My father is away abroad and I only have a mean old aunt who gives me about a penny a week! I hated to own up to such a miserable bit of money – and then one day I found a shilling belonging to some one and I bought something for somebody with it – and they were so terribly pleased – and I was so happy. I can't tell you how dreadful it is to want to be generous and not to be able to be!"

"Poor Kathleen!" said Isabel, and she patted her on the shoulder. "Nobody would have minded at all if only you had told them you hadn't any money. We could all have shared with you."

"But I was too proud to let you do that," said Kathleen. "And yet I wasn't too proud to steal. Oh, I can't think how I did it now! I took Janet's money – and Hilary's – and Belinda's. It was all so easy. And this afternoon I – I – I . . ."

She began to cry so bitterly that the twins were quite frightened. "Don't tell us if you'd rather not," said Pat.

"Oh, I'll tell you everything now I've begun," said poor Kathleen. "It's a relief to tell somebody. Well, this afternoon when I went to Rita's study, she wasn't there – but I saw her coat hanging up and her purse sticking out of it. And I went to it – and oh, Rita came in quietly and caught me! And she's going to Miss Theobald about it, and I shall be known all over the school as a thief, and I'll be expelled and . . ."

She wept again, and the twins looked at one another helplessly. They remembered all Kathleen's sudden generosity – her gifts – the marvellous cake with sugar roses on it – the fine chrysanthemums for Vera – and they remembered too Kathleen's flushed cheeks and shining eyes when she saw her friends enjoying the things she had bought for them.

"Kathleen – go and wash your face and come down to gym.," said Pat at last.

"I'm not going to," said Kathleen, obstinately. "I'm going to stay here and pack. I don't want to see anybody again. You two have been decent to me, but I know in your heart of hearts that you simply despise me!"

"We don't, Kath dear," said Isabel. "We're terribly, terribly sorry for you – and we do understand why you did it. You so badly wanted to be generous – you did a wrong thing to make a right thing, and that's never any good."

"Please go, and leave me alone," said Kathleen. "Please go."

The twins went out of the dormitory. Halfway to the gym. Isabel stopped and pulled at Pat's arm.

"Pat! Let's go and find Rita if we can. Let's say what we can for poor old Kathleen."

"All right," said Pat. The two of them went to Rita's study, but it was empty. "Blow!" said Pat. "I wonder if she's gone to Miss Theobald already."

"Well, come on – let's see," said Isabel. So to the Head's room they went – and coming out of the door, looking very grim indeed, was Rita George!

"What are you two kids doing here?" she said, and went on her way without waiting for an answer. Pat looked at Isabel.

"She's told Miss Theobald," she said. "Well – dare we go in and speak to the Head about it? I do really think Kathleen isn't an ordinary kind of thief – and if she gets branded as one, and sent away, she may really become one, and be spoilt for always. Come on – let's go in."

They knocked, and the Head called them to come in. She looked surprised to see them.

"Well, twins," she said. "What is the matter? You look rather serious."

Pat didn't quite know how to begin. Then the words came in a rush and the whole story came out about how Kathleen had stolen all the money, and why.

"But oh, Miss Theobald, Kathleen didn't spend a penny on herself," said Pat. "It was all for us others. She certainly took our money – but we got it back in gifts and things. She isn't just an ordinary, contemptible sort of thief. She's terribly, terribly upset. Oh, could you possibly do anything about it – not send her away – not let the school know? I'm quite sure Kathleen would try to repay every penny, and Isabel and I would help her all we could never to do such a thing again."

"You see, it was all because Kathleen got hardly any pocket-money and she was too proud to say so – and she hated to be thought mean and selfish because really she's terribly generous," said Isabel.

Miss Theobald smiled a very sweet smile at the earnest twins. "My dears," she said, "you tell me such a different story from Rita, and I'm so very glad to hear it. Rita naturally sees poor Kathleen as a plain thief. You see her as she is – a poor muddled child who wants to be generous and chooses an easy but a very wrong way. I am sure I would not have got any explanation from Kathleen, and I might have written to her aunt to take her away. And then I dread what might have happened to her, poor, sensitive child!"

"Oh, Miss Theobald! Do you mean that you will let Kathleen stay?" cried Pat.

"Of course," said the Head. "I must talk to her first, and get her to tell me all this herself. I shall know how to deal with her, don't worry. Where is she?"

"In her dormitory, packing," said Pat. Miss Theobald stood up. "I'll go to her," she said. "Now you go off to whatever lesson you are supposed to be at, and tell your teacher please to excuse your being late, but that you have been with me. And I just want to say this – I am proud of you both! You are kind and understanding, two things that matter a great deal."

Blushing with surprise and pleasure, the twins held open the door for Miss Theobald to go out. They looked at each other in delight.

"Isn't she a sport?" said Pat. "Oh, how glad I am we dared to come in and tell her. I believe things will be all right for Kath now!"

They sped off to gym., and were excused for being late. They wondered and wondered how Kathleen was getting on with Miss Theobald. They knew after tea when Kathleen, her eyes still red, but looking very much happier, came up to them.

"I'm not going," she said. "I'm going to stay here and show Miss Theobald I'm as decent as anyone else. She's going to write to my aunt and ask for a proper amount of pocket money to be paid to me – and I shall give back all the money I took – and start again. And if I can't be as generous as I'd like for a little while, I'll wait patiently till I can."

"Yes – and don't be afraid of owning up if you haven't got money to spare," said Pat. "Nobody minds that at all. That's just silly pride, to be afraid of saying when you can't afford something. Oh, Kath – I'm so glad you're not going. Isabel and I had just got to like you very much."

"You've been good friends to me," said Kathleen, squeezing their arms as she walked between them. "If ever I can return your kindness, I will. You *will* trust me again, won't you? It would be so awful not to be trusted. I couldn't bear that."

"Of course we'll trust you," said Pat. "If you go on like that I'll get a hundred pounds out of the bank and ask you to keep it for me! Don't be such a silly-billy!"

Miss Kennedy Again

The twins were really beginning to settle down well at St. Clare's. They were getting used to being in the lowest form instead of in the top one, and they were no longer called the "stuck-up twins". Mam'zelle had helped them a great deal with their French writing, and they had caught up with the rest of the form. Miss Roberts found that they had good brains and occasionally threw them a word of praise, which they treasured very much.

Kathleen was their firm friend. She really was a very generous-hearted girl, and although she now had no longer plenty of money to spend, she gave generously in other ways – mended Pat's stockings for her, stuck together a favourite vase of Mam'zelle's that got broken, and spent what time she could with Doris and Hilary when they had to go to the sick-room with "flu". She knew that she would never be dishonest again, and she held her head high and tried to forget the silly things she had done, which were now put right.

78

Miss Kennedy had a bit better time, for since she had been so nice over their Great Feast, the first-formers behaved better. But the second form were not so good. They had discovered that Miss Kennedy was terrified of cats, and it was perfectly astonishing the number of cats that appeared at times in the second-form classroom.

The second form found every cat they could lay hands on, and secreted them somewhere in the class-room before their history lesson. They had a big cupboard, and this was a good place to hide a cat.

One morning Miss Roberts was not well. She felt sure that she had "flu" coming, and she retired to bed, hoping to ward it off quickly. So poor Miss Kennedy had to tackle both first and second forms together. The first-formers went into the second-form classroom, as it was much bigger than theirs.

They entered in an orderly line. Miss Jenks, the second-form mistress, was there, and she gave them their places. "Now sit quietly till Miss Kennedy comes," she said, and went off to take needlework with another form.

As soon as she had gone, a perfect babel of noise broke out, and to the enormous astonishment of the first-formers, a large black cat was produced from the passage, where Tessie, a girl of the second form, had hidden the cat in a cupboard.

The cat was most amiable. It arched its back and purred, sticking its tail up in the air. The twins stared at it in surprise.

"Why the cat?" asked Pat. "Is it a member of your class, by any chance?"

"Ha ha! Funny joke, I don't think," said Pam, stroking the cat. "No, Pat – It's just going to give old Kenny a fine surprise, that's all! Didn't you know she was terrified of cats? We're going to shut old Blackie up in our handwork cupboard over there – and then, at a good

79

moment Tessie, who sits near, is going to pull the door open – and out will walk dear old Blackie, large as life and twice as natural – and he'll make straight for Kenny, you see if he doesn't!"

The first-formers began to giggle. This was marvellous – even better than fire-cracks!

"Sh! She's coming!" came a cry from the door, where some one was keeping guard. "To your places! Put the cat into the cupboard, quick, Tessie!"

The cat went into the cupboard with a rush, much to its amazement. The door was shut on it. Kathleen, who was passionately fond of animals, began to object.

"I say – can the cat breathe properly in there? Ought we to . . ."

"Shut up!" hissed Tessie, and at that moment in walked Miss Kennedy, her pile of books under her arm. She smiled at the girls and sat down. She felt very nervous, for she did not like handling two forms at once. Also she felt something was in the air, and did not like the one or two chuckles that she heard from the back row. Her book dropped to the floor and she bent to pick it up – and her belt snapped undone, and flew off.

This really wasn't very funny, but it seemed most humorous to the girls in the front row, and they bent over their books, trying not to laugh. Miss Kennedy knew that they were laughing and she determined to be firm for once.

"Any girl who disturbs the class by laughing or playing will stand the whole of the time," she announced in as firm a voice as she could. Every one was astonished to hear the mild Miss Kennedy make such a statement, and for a while the lesson went smoothly.

Tessie was to let the cat out about half-way through the class – but the cat thought otherwise. It had lain down on the handwork, and had got itself mixed up with the coloured raffia that was used by the girls for their basket-making. It tried to lick the raffia off its back legs, but couldn't.

It stood up and shook itself. It turned round and round – but the more it turned, the more entangled it got, and at last it became frightened.

It jumped about on the shelf, and some curious noises came from the cupboard. At first Miss Kennedy could not imagine what the noise was. The girls knew quite well that it was the cat, and they bent their heads over their exercise books, doing their best not to laugh.

The cat got excited. It leapt into the air and knocked its head against the shelf above. Then it scrabbled about and bit savagely at the entangling raffia.

"What *is* in that cupboard?" said Miss Kennedy at last.

"The handwork, Miss Kennedy," answered Tessie.

"I know that," answered Miss Kennedy, impatiently. "But handwork doesn't make a noise. What *can* be causing all that disturbance? It must be mice."

It certainly wasn't mice. It was just poor old Blackie going completely mad. He tore round and round the big shelf, the raffia catching his legs all the time. The whole class began to giggle helplessly.

"This is too much!" said Miss Kennedy, angrily. She walked quickly to the handwork cupboard and flung open the door. Blackie was thrilled, and leapt out with an enormous yowl. Miss Kennedy gave a shriek when she saw the big black animal springing out, and she rushed to the door. Blackie went with her, thinking she was going to let him out. He rubbed against her ankles and Miss Kennedy went white with fright, for she really was quite terrified of cats.

Blackie and Miss Kennedy went out of the door together, parted, and fled in opposite directions. The girls put down their heads on their desks and almost sobbed with laughter. Tears trickled out of Kathleen's eyes, and as for the twins, they had to hold their sides, for they each got dreadful stitches with laughing so much.

Tessie staggered to the door and shut it, in case any other mistress came by. For at least five minutes the girls let themselves go and laughed till they cried. As soon as they stopped, some one started them off again.

"Oh, I say – *did* you see Blackie when he shot out?" cried Tessie, and every one giggled again.

"It must be mice!" said Doris, imitating Miss Kennedy's voice. Shrieks of laughter again.

"Sh!" said Tessie, wiping her eyes. "Some one will hear us. I say – I wonder what's become of old Kenny? She disappeared into the blue. Do you suppose she'll come back and finish the lesson?"

But no Miss Kennedy came back. She was sitting in one of the empty common rooms, drinking a glass of water, and looking very pale. She was afraid of cats as some people are afraid of beetles or bats – but that was not all that made her feel worried and ill. It was the thought of the girls playing the trick on her, knowing that she would so easily fall into the trap.

"I'm absolutely no good at taking a class," thought Miss Kennedy, putting down her glass. "It was all very well when I coached one or two girls at a time – but this job is too much for me. And yet the money does come in so useful now. Mother is ill. Still, it's no use. I must give it up."

She decided to go down to the town and meet a friend of hers at tea-time. She would talk over the matter with her, then come back and give in her notice to Miss Theobald, confessing that she could neither teach nor keep discipline.

So down to the town she went at four o'clock, after telephoning to her friend, Miss Roper, to meet her at the tea-shop.

Miss Kennedy shrieked when she saw the cat

And to the same shop went the twins and Kathleen, having tea there by themselves as a great treat! The tea-shop was divided into little cosy partitions with red curtains, and the three girls were already sitting eating buttered buns when Miss Kennedy and Miss Roper came in.

They chose the partition next to the three girls, and sat down. The girls could not see them – but it was possible to hear the voices. And they recognized Miss Kennedy's at once!

"Listen! There's old Kenny! I bet she's going to talk about the black cat!" chuckled Kathleen. The girls had no intention of eavesdropping, but they could not help hearing what was said. And, as they thought, Kenny began to talk about the morning's happenings.

But she talked of something else too – of her old mother, ill and poor; of the money that her teaching had so unexpectedly brought in; of the bills she had to pay. She spoke with sadness of her failure to hold the girls in class.

"I'm a fraud," she told her friend. "I take the school's money for teaching the girls, and I don't teach them a thing, because I can't manage them, and they just rag me the whole time. Don't you think I should tell the head this, Clara? It's not honest of me to go on, leaving my classes because they rag me. Miss Lewis, the school's history specialist, can't possibly come back till the end of next term – but I don't see how I can honestly take her place till then."

"But you do so badly need the money to help your mother whilst she's ill," said Miss Roper. "It's bad luck, my dear – those girls must be wretches."

The three girls listened, stricken dumb. They were horrified. What seemed just teasing and ragging to them, meant losing a job to somebody else, meant being a failure – not being able to help a mother when she was ill.

"Let's go," muttered Pat, in a low voice. "We oughtn't to overhear this."

They crept out, unseen by Miss Kennedy, paid their bill and went back to school. They all felt unhappy. They couldn't let Miss Kennedy give up her post. She *was* a silly in many ways, but she was kind, and a real sport. And they, the girls, *were* wretches!

"Oh, dash, I do feel mean!" said Kathleen, sitting down in their common room. "I just hate myself now. I loved the joke this morning – but a joke's not a joke when it means real unhappiness to somebody else."

"We can't let Kenny go to Miss Theobald," said Pat, suddenly. "It would look awful. Look here – we've got to do something, for goodness sake. Think hard!"

Isabel looked up. "There's only one thing to do, really," she said. "We ought to get all our form to sign a letter, and the second form too, apologizing for the trick, and swearing we won't rag Kenny again. And we'll have to stick to that."

"That's not a bad idea at all," said Pat. "Kath, you go to the second form – they're having a meeting – and tell them quite shortly what's happened. I'll write out the letter – and each one of us can sign it."

Kathleen sped off. Pat took a pen and some notepaper, and she and Isabel wrote out the letter. This is what it said:

DEAR MISS KENNEDY,

We are all ashamed of our behaviour this morning, and we do ask you to accept our very humble apologies. We didn't mean the cat to jump out at you. Please forgive us. If you will, we promise never to rag you again, but to behave much better, and work hard. We thought

you were a great sport not to split on us about You
Know What.

Yours sincerely,

and then all the names of the girls were to follow, written
out by each girl.

The second form came in to sign their names.
"What's 'You Know What'?" asked Tessie, curiously.

"It's our Great Midnight Feast," answered Pat. "She
knew we had one and didn't tell. Now, has every one
signed? You haven't, Lorna. Put your name at the
bottom."

All the girls felt rather ashamed when they heard
Kathleen's tale of what they had overheard.

"You shouldn't really have listened," said Hilary, re-
provingly. "It's mean to overhear things."

"I know," said Pat. "But we really couldn't help it,
Hilary. And anyway, I'm glad we did. We can stop Kenny giving up her job, anyway."

It did prevent Miss Kennedy from going to Miss
Theobald when she came in that evening. She saw the
letter on her desk, and opened it. When she read it, the
tears came into her eyes.

"What a nice letter!" she thought. "The girls are not
little wretches after all! If only they keep their promise! I should be happy teaching them then!"

She thanked each form the next morning, and as-
sured them that she forgave them. And, for the first
time that term, her lessons went as smoothly as those
of the other teachers, for the girls had no intention of
breaking their word.

There would be giggles now and then – sly flippings
of paper darts – but no organized ragging, and no un-
kindness. Kenny was happy. She taught well now that
she had no ragging to fight, and the girls became interested and keen.

"I'm glad we did the decent thing," said Pat, one day, after the history lesson. "I asked old Kenny how her mother was today, and she said she's much better, and is coming out of the nursing home tomorrow. Wouldn't it have been awful if she had died because we made Kenny lose her job so that her mother couldn't be nursed back to health?"

"*Awful*," agreed Isabel. And every one in the form thought the same.

A Broken Window

One morning Hilary came into the common room most excited.

"I say! Did you know that the circus was coming to the field just outside the town? Well, it is! I saw the notices up!"

"Golly! I hope we're all allowed to go!" said Pat, who loved a circus.

"It's Galliano's Circus," said Hilary, and she pulled a handbill out of her pocket. "Look – clowns, acrobats, dancing horses, performing dogs, everything. If only Miss Theobald gives permission for the school to go!"

Miss Theobald did. She said that each evening two of the forms might go, with their teachers. The first form were thrilled. Pat, Isabel, Kathleen and Janet went down to the town to examine the big coloured posters pasted up everywhere.

They did look exciting. Then the girls went to see the big tents set up in the field. They leaned over the gate and watched the sleek satin-skinned horses being galloped round, and saw five clumsy-looking bears ambling along with their trainer. They watched in wonder when a big chimpanzee dressed up in trousers and jersey, came along hand in hand with a small boy, who had a terrier at his heels.

"Gracious! Look at that big monkey!" cried Isabel.

"Sammy's not a monkey. He's a chimpanzee," said the boy, smiling. "Shake hands, Sammy!"

The big chimpanzee solemnly held out his hand to the girls. Isabel and Kathleen were too afraid to take it, but Pat put out her hand at once. Sammy shook it up and down.

"Are you coming to see our show?" asked the boy.

"Rather!" said Pat. "Are you in the circus? What do you do?"

"I'm Jimmy Brown, and I go into the ring with my famous dog, Lucky. That's Lucky, just by your feet. She knows how to spell and count!"

"Oh, no! Dogs can't do that!" said Isabel.

Jimmy laughed. "Well, mine can. You'll see when you come! Look – see that girl over there, riding the black horse – that's Lotta. You'll see her in the ring too. She can ride the wildest horse in the world!"

The girls stared at Lotta. She was galloping round the field on a beautiful black horse. As she came near she suddenly stood up on the horse's back and waved to the astonished girls!

"Isn't she awfully clever!" said Pat. "How I wish I could ride like that! Doesn't she ever fall off?"

"Of course not," said Jimmy. "Well, I must go. Come on, Sammy. We'll look out for you four girls when you come to the show!"

He went off with the chimpanzee and the little dog. The girls made their way back to school. They were longing for the night to come when they might go to the circus with the first and second forms.

"There are two shows each night," said Pat. "One at 6.30 to 8.30, and the second at 8.45 to 10.45. I wish we were going to the later one – it would be sport getting back at eleven o'clock!"

"No such luck," said Isabel. "Come on, hurry – we shall be late for tea."

But a dreadful blow befell the first form the next morning. They came into their classroom, chattering as usual – and saw that one big pane of the middle window was completely broken! Miss Roberts was at her desk, looking stern.

"Gracious! How did the window get broken?" cried Janet in surprise.

"That is exactly what I would like to know," said Miss Roberts. "When I was in the common room I heard a crash, and came to see what caused it. I heard the sound of running feet going round the corner of the corridor – and when I came into the room I saw the broken window!"

"Who did it?" said Pat.

"I don't know," answered Miss Roberts. "But this is what broke the window." She held up a hard rubber lacrosse ball. "I found it still rolling across the floor when I came in. Somebody must have been playing with it in the classroom – and the window was smashed. It's against the rules to take lacrosse balls out of the locker in the gym, unless you go to games, as you know."

Every one listened in silence. They all felt a little guilty when Miss Roberts mentioned that it was against the rules to take lacrosse balls, because it was a rule nobody bothered to keep. Any girl slipped to the locker to borrow a ball to play with at break.

"Now," said Miss Roberts, "I want the girl who broke the window to own up now, or to come to me at break and tell me then. She should, of course, have stayed to own up as soon as the window was broken – but it is quite natural in a moment of fright to run away."

Nobody spoke. All the girls sat perfectly still in their

seats. Nobody looked at any one else. Miss Roberts looked searchingly along the rows, looking for a guilty face.

But as half the girls were blushing with sheer nervousness, that was no help. Practically all the class looked guilty and ill at ease. They always did when anything went wrong.

"Well," said Miss Roberts at last, "it is quite evident that the culprit is not going to own up now. She must come to me at break, without fail. All you girls have a sense of honour, I know, and not one of you is a coward. So I am quite sure that the culprit will be brave enough to come to me. I shall be in the common room, alone."

Still nobody said a word. One or two looked round at each other, and every one wondered who the sinner was. Pat and Isabel smiled nervously at each other. They had been together since breakfast, so they knew that neither of *them* was the sinner!

The first lesson began. It was maths. Miss Roberts was not in a good temper, and nobody dared to utter a word. Dark and fair heads were bent busily over books, and when the form-mistress rapped out an order it was obeyed at once. Every one knew how dangerous it would be to get into trouble when Miss Roberts was on the warpath.

After maths. came French. Mam'zelle came into the room, and exclaimed at the broken window.

"*Tiens!* The window is broken! How did that happen?"

"We don't know, Mam'zelle," said Hilary. "Nobody has owned up yet."

"That is abominable!" cried Mam'zelle, looking round the class with her big dark eyes. "It is not brave!"

The class said nothing. They all felt uncomfortable,

for it was not nice to think that somebody in the class was a coward. Still, maybe the culprit would own up at break. Whoever could it be?

Pat and Isabel thought hard. It couldn't be Janet or Hilary, for both girls were brave-spirited and owned to a fault at once. It couldn't be Kathleen, for she had been with them. It might be Vera – or Sheila – or Joan – or Doris. No, surely it couldn't be any of them! They wouldn't be cowards.

At break the first form got together and discussed the matter. "It wasn't *us*," said Pat. "Isabel and I were together all the time after breakfast till we went to the class-room. And Kathleen was with us too."

"Well, it wasn't *me*," said Hilary. "I was doing a job for Rita."

"And it wasn't *me*," said Janet. "I was cleaning the bird-table, and Doris was helping."

One by one the girls of the first form all said what they had been doing between breakfast-time and the first lesson. Apparently not one of them could have broken the window – though one must be telling an untruth!

After break the girls took their places in their form room. Miss Roberts came in, her mouth in a thin line and her hazel eyes cold. She looked round the class.

"I am sorry to say that no one has owned up," she said. "So I have had to report the matter to Miss Theobald. She agrees with me that the window must be paid for by the whole class, as the culprit hasn't owned up. The window is made of vita-glass, and will cost twenty shillings to mend. Miss Theobald has decided instead of letting you go to the circus, which would cost one shilling each, she will use the money for the window."

There was a gasp of dismay from all the girls. Not go to the circus! That was a terrible blow. They looked round one another, angry and upset. Why should the whole class suffer because one person had done a wrong thing? It didn't seem fair.

"I am sure that the one who broke the window will not want her whole class to be punished," went on Miss Roberts. "So I hope she will still own up, before the night comes when our form is due to go to the show – that is, on Thursday. And I trust that if any of you know who it is you will insist that she does her duty by her form."

"But Miss Roberts, suppose nobody owns up," began Hilary, "couldn't we all put a shilling of our own towards the window and still go to the circus?"

"No," said Miss Roberts. "There's no argument, Hilary. What I have said, stands, and will not be altered. Open your books at page eighty-two, please."

What a babel there was after morning school was over, in the quarter of an hour before dinner! How angry and indignant the girls were!

"It's a shame!" cried Janet. "I didn't do it – nor did you, Pat and Isabel – and we jolly well know it. So why should we be punished too?"

"Well, it's the custom in schools to make a whole form suffer for one person in a case like this," said Hilary. "They do it at my brother's school too – though it doesn't happen often. I don't see the point of it myself, but there you are. If only I knew who it was! Wouldn't I take them by the scruff of the neck and give them a shaking!"

"Look here – what about one of us owning up to it, so that the rest can go?" said Kathleen, suddenly. "I don't mind owning up and taking the blame. Then all you others can go."

"Don't be an idiot," said Pat, slipping her arm through Kathleen's. "As if we'd let you do a thing like that!"

"I suppose you *didn't* do it, Kath?" said Sheila, half-laughing.

"Of course she didn't!" cried Isabel. "She was with Pat and me all the time. It's jolly decent of her to offer to take the blame – but I wouldn't dream of it. If I heard she'd owned up to save our skins I'd go straight to Miss Roberts myself and tell her that Kathleen couldn't possibly have done it!"

"Oh, well," said Kathleen, "I shan't say anything, of course, if you feel like that about it. If only we knew which of us had done it!"

The whole of Tuesday slipped by and the whole of Wednesday. Still nobody had owned up. When Thursday came Miss Roberts informed the class that the second form were to go to the circus, but not the first. The class groaned and fidgeted.

"I'm very sorry," said Miss Roberts. "It's most unfortunate. I only hope that the culprit is feeling most unhappy and uncomfortable. Now, no more groaning, please. Let's get on with our geography!"

The Four Truants

That afternoon, after tea, four girls of the first form held a secret meeting in one of the little music rooms. They were the twins, and Kathleen and Janet. They were all furious because they were not allowed to go that night to the show in the town.

"Look here! *Let's* go!" said Janet. "We can slip off at a quarter past eight on our bikes without any one noticing, if we go down the path by the lacrosse field. And we can get back in the dark all right."

"But the school doors are locked at ten," said Kathleen.

"I know that, idiot!" said Janet. "But what's the matter with a ladder? There's one alongside the gardener's shed. We can easily get into our dormitory window with that."

"Yes – but the ladder will be seen the next morning, leading up to our window!" said Isabel.

"Oh, golly, haven't you *any* brains!" sighed Janet. *"One* of us can go up the ladder – and undo the side-door to let the others in – and we can all take the ladder back to the shed before we go in. Is that quite clear, or shall I say it all over again?"

Every one laughed. Janet was funny when she was impatient. "I see," said Pat. "But gosh, if we were caught! I don't like to think what would happen to us."

"Well, don't," said Janet, "because we *shan't* be caught! Miss Roberts never puts the light on at night when she comes to our dormitory now. We shall be all right. We must tell Hilary though. She won't come with us because she's head-girl and keeps all the rules – but she won't stop us going."

Hilary didn't stop them. "All right," she said. "Risk it if you want to. I won't stop you. But for goodness' sake don't get caught!"

The second form went off to the circus with Miss Jenks. The first form stayed behind, sulky and angry. Only the four who were going to slip off by themselves looked at all bright. Most of the first form knew what Janet had planned, but nobody else dared to risk it.

"You'll get expelled if you're caught, I shouldn't wonder," said Doris.

"We shan't be expelled and we shan't be caught," said Janet, firmly.

When the time came, the four girls put on their hats and coats and slipped down to the side-door. It was dark outside, but the night was clear. Coming home there would be a moon. They went softly to the bicycle shed.

"Golly! What a noise bikes make!" whispered Janet, as the four machines clanked and rattled. "Now – down the path by the field. Come on."

Off they all rode, their lamps shining in the darkness. When they arrived at the circus field they saw the people streaming out of the gates. They had been to the 6.30 performance.

"Look out! Hide by the hedge till every one's gone!" said Janet. "We don't want to run into Miss Jenks!"

They hid until it was safe. They pushed their bicycles behind the hedge and went to the gate, where people were already going in, under the flare of acetylene lamps. The girls paid and went towards the big circus tent. Soon they had taken their seats, well at the back in case any one saw them. They took off their school hats.

The circus was marvellous. They saw the girl Lotta, now dressed in a sparkling, shining frock, riding bare-back round the ring, standing on her horse, kneeling, jumping, smiling all the time. They saw Jimmy and his dog Lucky, and could not imagine how he had been trained to be so clever. They cheered the absurd clowns and the amazing acrobats. They loved big Mr. Galliano, with his cracking whip and big moustaches. It was a gorgeous show and the four girls enjoyed every minute.

"We'd better slip out a bit before the end," whispered Janet, watching Sammy the chimpanzee solemnly undress himself and put on a pair of pyjamas. "I say – isn't he funny? Oh, look – he's getting into bed!"

Just before the show was finished the girls slipped out quietly. Everyone was intent on watching the five bears, who were now playing ring-a-ring-of-roses with their trainer.

"*All* fall down!" chanted the trainer, and just as the four girls went out, down fell the five bears in the ring, for all the world as if they were children!

"What a marvellous show!" said Janet, as they made their way to where they had left their bicycles. "Where's my bike? Oh, here it is."

They mounted their bicycles and rode off. The moon was up now and they could see clearly. They were soon back at the school. They put their bicycles into the shed as quietly as they could, and then, with beating hearts, they tiptoed to the shed, outside which the ladder was kept.

They all felt excited and nervous. Just suppose they were caught now! It would be awful. But nobody was about. A dim light showed from a mistress's bedroom in the eastern wing of the school. It was about eleven o'clock, and all the girls and some of the mistresses would be asleep.

They looked for the ladder. There were two, a small one and a much bigger one. Janet tugged at the smaller one.

"I should think this one will just about reach," she said. So the four of them carried it to where their dormitory windows shone in the moonlight. They kept in the dark shadows and were as quiet as they could be.

They set the ladder up gently against the wall – but to their great dismay it didn't nearly reach to the window-sill!

"Dash!" said Janet. "Look at that! It's much too dangerous to try and climb to the sill from the top of the ladder – it's so far below the window. Well – come on, let's take it back and get the other ladder. That's long enough to reach to the roof, I should think!"

They took the small ladder back and put it down gently. But then they found they could not possibly carry the big ladder! It was enormously heavy and needed two or three gardeners to handle it. The four girls could hardly move it and certainly would not be able to set it up against the wall.

They stood in the moonlight and stared at one another in dismay. "Now what are we going to do?" asked Isabel, her voice quivering. "We can't stay out here all night."

"Of course not, silly," said Janet. "We'll try all the doors. Maybe we'll find one that's unlocked. Cheer up."

So they tiptoed round the school, trying the doors, but every one of them was safely locked and bolted. The maids did their work well!

Kathleen began to cry. She did not want to be caught breaking the rules, because she had tried very hard to be in Miss Theobald's good books since she had been forgiven for her fault. It suddenly seemed a very dreadful thing to her to be out of doors when all the others were in bed and asleep.

"We shall be discovered in the morning," she whispered. "And we shall catch our deaths of cold staying out here."

"Shut up and don't be such a baby," said Janet fiercely.

"I know what we can do! We'll throw little pebbles up to our dormitory window!" said Pat. "They will make a rattling noise and maybe one of the girls will wake. Then she can slip down and open a door for us."

"Good idea!" said Janet. "Pick up tiny pebbles, every one!"

They scooped handfuls up from the gravel, and threw them up. But Kathleen threw very badly and her pebbles rattled against the wrong window – the one above the dormitory, where Mam'zelle slept! And Mam'zelle awoke!

"Quick! Back into the shadows!" whispered Janet, urgently. "Idiot – you hit Mam'zelle's window!"

The big dark head of Mam'zelle looked out, and they heard her mutter to herself. They squeezed together in a corner, hardly daring to breathe, terrified that Mamzelle would see them. But the shadows were black and she could see nothing. Puzzled, and yawning deeply, she went back to her bed. The girls stayed where they were for a few minutes and then began to whisper.

"This is awful! Really awful. What *are* we going to do?"

"I do wish we hadn't slipped off to the circus!"

"I'm so cold my teeth are chattering."

Then Pat clutched hold of Isabel's arm and whispered loudly. "Look – look – isn't that some one looking out of our dormitory window?"

They all looked up – and sure enough a girl's head was peeping from the window. Pat slipped out of the shadows and stood in the moonlight. Hilary's voice came down to her in a whisper.

"Pat! How late you are! Where are the others?"

"Here," whispered Pat. "The ladders aren't any good. Open the side-door here and let us in, Hilary, quick! We're so cold."

Hilary drew in her head and disappeared. A minute later the four girls heard the key turning in the lock of the side-door, and the bolts being slipped back – and the door was open! They crept in quietly and Hilary locked and bolted the door once more.

They all slipped upstairs like mice, and tip-toed in their stockinged feet to their dormitory. Once there they sank on to Janet's bed and began to giggle from sheer excitement and relief.

They told Hilary all that had happened, Doris woke up and joined the little group. The four truants began to feel much better now that they were safe, and boasted of all they had done.

"Did you hear our pebbles rattling on the window?" asked Janet of Hilary. "Why did you come to the window? Golly, wasn't I glad to hear your voice?"

"Your pebbles came rattling on to the floor!" said

Hilary, with a laugh. "The window was open at the bottom. I left it like that for you to climb in. When I heard the sound of pebbles all over the lino I woke up. At first I couldn't imagine what the noise was – then I switched on my torch and saw the bits of gravel. We'll have to sweep those up in the morning."

Janet yawned. "I'm so tired," she said. "The circus was marvellous. I wish you could have seen it, Hilary."

"So do I," said Hilary. "Buck up and get undressed now, for goodness' sake. And don't make too much noise or you'll wake Mam'zelle. Her room's just above, remember."

"We know that all right!" said Pat, giggling as she remembered Mam'zelle's dark head sticking out of the window. "Where's my nightie? Oh, blow, where's it gone?"

"You won't find it on *my* bed, silly," said Isabel, who was already undressed and in her nightgown. "You've got muddled. That's your bed, over there, and there's your nightie on the pillow."

"Oh, yes," said Pat, yawning. "I wish I could go to sleep in my clothes!"

Soon all the dormitory was quiet once more, and every girl was asleep. The four truants slept peacefully – but there was a shock in store for them in the morning!

A Great Disappointment

The four truants were extremely sleepy the next day. They could hardly wake up. When the dressing-bell went not one of them got out of bed.

"Hi, Janet! Kathleen! Aren't you going to get a move on?" cried Hilary. "You'll be late. And just look at those lazy twins – they haven't even opened their eyes!"

"Another five minutes!" murmured Pat, sleepily. But the five minutes stretched into ten, and still the four girls hadn't moved. Hilary winked at Doris, and the two of them went swiftly to the four white beds and stripped off all the bedclothes, throwing them on the floor.

"Oooooh!" shivered the girls, for it was a very cold morning. "You mean things!"

"Come on, get up, or you'll get into a row," said Hilary. And, very slowly and sleepily the four dressed, yawning all the time. They cheered up a bit when the rest of the form clustered round them, asking what happened the night before. They really felt almost heroines as they related their exciting adventures.

"I don't feel in the least like lessons this morning," said Janet. "Oh, my goodness – Miss Roberts is taking us for algebra, isn't she? I always am stupid about that anyhow, and I shan't be able to understand a thing to-day. I hope she's in a good temper."

The class went into their form room, and took their places. Janet got out her algebra book and hurriedly glanced through the chapter she had been told to learn. It seemed to her as if she had entirely forgotten every word! But that was just because she had had such a short night.

"Here comes Miss Roberts!" hissed Doris, who was at the door. The girls stood. Miss Roberts came in – and goodness, whatever could have happened! She looked very pleased, and her eyes sparkled so that she looked really pretty.

"Sit, girls," she said, and the girls sat down, wondering why their mistress looked so pleased. Had they done some marvellous prep. or something?

"Girls," said Miss Roberts, "I feel very happy about something this morning. I have found out that it was not any one in my form who broke the window!"

The girls looked at her, amazed. Miss Roberts smiled round the class.

"It was one of the second form," she said. "Apparently the ball bounced in here, the girl rushed for it, tried to catch it, and it was knocked on to the window, which broke."

"But why didn't she own up?" cried Hilary, indignantly. "That was jolly mean of her! We missed going to the circus because of that."

"Wait," said Miss Roberts. "The girl was Queenie Hobart, who, as you know, is now in the sick-room with a bad attack of 'flu'. She was frightened when she broke the window, but meant to own up at the end of the morning. In the middle of the morning she was taken ill and was hurried off to the sick-room where she has been really ill for a few days. Today she is better, and her form-mistress, Miss Jenks, went to see her."

"Did she own up then?" asked Janet.

"Miss Jenks told her that the second form had gone to the circus the night before, but not the first form, and Queenie asked why," said Miss Roberts. "When she heard that you had all been punished for something that was her fault, she was very upset and began to cry. She told Miss Jenks, of course, and Miss Jenks came hurrying to tell me."

"Oh! I *am* glad it wasn't anybody in our form," said Hilary. "I did hate to think that somebody was such a mean coward!"

"And I couldn't understand it either," said Miss Roberts. "I think I know you all pretty well – and although you are sometimes very stupid, aggravating and, in fact, a set of nuisances – I really couldn't believe that any of you were cowards!"

Miss Roberts smiled as she made these remarks, and the class laughed. They were all most relieved.

"Can we go to the circus after all, then?" asked Hilary.

"There's still tonight or tomorrow."

"Of course," said Miss Roberts. "You are to go tomorrow, Miss Theobald says – and to make up for your disappointment, which was quite undeserved, I am to take you down into the town and give you a real good tea first! What do you think of that?"

The girls thought a lot of it! They said "Oooh" and "Ah!" and rubbed their hands together, and looked as cheerful as possible. Tea first – a really scrumptious tea – and then the circus – and it was sure to be good fun on the last night of all! What luck that Queenie had owned up in time!

But there were four girls who were feeling most uncomfortable about the whole thing – and they were the twins, and Kathleen and Janet. They had played truant and seen the show! They looked at one another and felt very guilty. Why hadn't they waited?

They went to Hilary about it afterwards. "Hilary! We feel awfully mean now somehow – do you think we ought to go tomorrow?" asked Pat.

"Well, if you don't, what excuse will you make?" said Hilary. "Since you ask me, I say you jolly well oughtn't to go! You've had your pleasure, by breaking the rules – well, every one breaks rules sometimes, so I'm not blaming you for that. The thing is, it's not fair that you should have a second treat. I should feel like that myself, just as you do. But if you go and tell Miss Roberts why, you certainly will get into a first-class row."

"Could we say we don't feel well?" said Isabel. "I really don't feel awfully well today – I had so little sleep."

"Well, say that tomorrow," said Hilary. "But I say, it's bad luck on you, isn't it! You've done yourself out of a gorgeous tea, and every one knows that a Saturday night is the best night to see a show."

"I wish we hadn't been so impatient now," sighed

Kathleen. "I would so love to go with you tomorrow."

The four were very sad. They talked about it together. "Let's go anyhow!" said Janet. Then almost immediately she changed her mind. "No, we can't. I'd feel mean all the time. And the other girls would think us mean too."

"I only hope Miss Roberts doesn't send us to Matron for some of her disgusting medicine, when we tell her we don't feel well tomorrow," said Kathleen, who was a perfect coward over taking medicine.

But when the next day came there was no question of telling a story about feeling unwell – for all four girls had bad colds! They had caught a chill standing about waiting to get into the school on Thursday night – and how they sneezed and coughed!

Miss Roberts noticed at once. "You'd better spend a day in bed," she said. "You may be in for 'flu'. Go along to Matron and ask her to take your temperatures. Four of you at once! Wherever could you all have caught such bad colds?"

They didn't tell her. They went to Matron, feeling very sad and sorry. Kathleen had a temperature, and as Matron was not at all sure that the whole lot were not going to have "flu" she did the sensible thing and popped them all into bed. She gave them each a dose out of one of her enormous bottles, tucked them up, and left them in the sick-room together.

"A-tish-oo!" sneezed Kathleen. "Golly, weren't we idiots to rush off like that the other night. I do hate having a beastly cold like this."

"And missing that tea," sighed Pat. "Hilary said Miss Roberts had rung up the tea-shop and made sure that they had those special chocolate cakes we like."

"Well – it's no use grumbling!" said Isabel, sensibly. "We brought this on ourselves. Now shut up, you others. I want to read."

103

The first form went off at five with Miss Roberts and had a gorgeous tea. Miss Roberts bought four of the special chocolate cakes to take back to the girls in the sick-room.

"I think they have been perfect bricks about all this," she said to Hilary. "Not a grumble, not one word of complaint!"

Hilary said nothing. Miss Roberts would have been astonished if she had known the real reason why the four truants were not at the circus! But Hilary was certainly not going to tell her.

The circus was at its best that night – and afterwards the girls were allowed to go behind the ring and see the performers at close quarters. Sammy the chimpanzee was delighted to see them and kept taking off his cap to them most politely. Jumbo, the enormous elephant, blew down Hilary's neck and lifted her curls as if they had been blown by the wind! Lotta let them all stroke her magnificent horse, Black Beauty. Altogether, it was a marvellous evening, the girls went back tired, but very happy and talkative.

Miss Roberts slipped into the sick-room to see if the four girls were awake. Matron was just tucking them up for the night.

"There's nothing much wrong with them," she told Miss Roberts. "Kathleen's temperature is down to normal. They've just got ordinary bad colds, that's all. As tomorrow is Sunday I'll keep them in bed one more day."

"I've brought them some of the special chocolate cakes we always have at the tea-shop," said Miss Roberts. "I suppose they mustn't have them now."

"Oh, they can if they feel like it," said Matron, smiling. "It won't hurt them!"

All four girls felt like chocolate cakes immediately, and sat up. They thought it was jolly kind of Miss Roberts to think of them. They munched their cakes and listened to their teacher's recital of the evening's happenings.

"Didn't you think Sammy the chimpanzee was funny when he undressed himself and got into bed?" asked Kathleen eagerly, quite forgetting that Miss Roberts had no idea she had seen the circus. Miss Roberts stared in surprise.

"Kathleen saw the posters in the town," said Pat, hurriedly, glaring at the unfortunate Kathleen with rage.

"I think it's time the girls settled down now, Miss Roberts," said Matron, coming in, luckily for the four, at that very moment. Miss Roberts said good night at once, and went. They girls lay down, whilst Matron fussed round a bit, then turned out the light, and went.

"Idiot, Kathleen!" said Janet. "You nearly gave us all away!"

"Sorry," said Kathleen, sleepily. "I quite forgot!"

"No more talking!" said Matron, putting her head round the door. "Another word, and I'll come in and give you all a dose of my very nastiest medicine!"

And after that there wasn't a word!

A Terrible Quarrel

The weeks went quickly by. Half-term came and went. The twins' mother came to see them at half-term and took them out in the car for the day. She was glad to see them looking so well and happy.

"Well, how are you getting on?" she asked. "I hope you're not finding St. Clare's quite as bad as you feared!"

The twins blushed. "It's not a bad school," said Pat.

"It's quite decent," said Isabel. Their mother smiled to herself. She knew the twins so well – and their few words meant that they liked St. Clare's and were happy.

Every week there were lacrosse matches. Sometimes they were played by the lower forms, sometimes by the upper. The twins became very keen indeed, and used to watch all the upper form matches with great enjoyment. They thought Belinda Towers was marvellous. She was as swift as the wind, and her catching was beautiful to watch.

"Do you remember how rude we were to her at the beginning of the term?" said Pat. "Golly, I wonder how we dared now!"

"We were awful idiots," said Isabel. "Honestly, I wonder how everyone put up with us!"

"Well, there's one person I simply *can't* put up with!" said Pat. "And that's Sheila Naylor. What *is* the matter with her? She's so awfully haughty and conceited – always talking about her marvellous home and the number of servants they keep, and her horse, and their three motor-cars. Always pushing herself forward and airing her opinions – which aren't worth twopence, anyway!"

Everyone found Sheila very trying indeed. She was always doing her best to impress people, and to make them think that she was wonderful. Actually she was a plain and ordinary girl, with rather bad manners, who didn't speak very well. All her clothes were good, and she went to no end of trouble to buy the best of everything – and yet she never brushed her hair really well, and if she could forget to wash her neck, she would!

The most impatient girl in the first form was Janet. She could not bear vanity, or conceit, and Sheila's airs and graces irritated her beyond words. She hadn't the patience to put up with Sheila, and usually Sheila knew this and kept out of her way.

One afternoon, just before tea, the first form were enjoying themselves in their common room. Pat put on the gramophone, and played the same record four times running. Janet looked up.

"For goodness' sake! Are you trying to learn that record by heart, Pat? Take it off and break it! If I have to hear it again I'll scream!"

"You didn't ought to talk like that," began Sheila, in a mincing voice – and Janet flung down her book in a rage.

"Hark at Sheila! 'Didn't ought to!' Good heavens, Sheila, where were you brought up? Haven't you learnt by now that decent people don't say 'Didn't ought to!' My goodness, you talk about your servants, and your Rolls Royce cars, your horse and your lake and goodness knows what – and then you talk like the daughter of the dustman!"

Sheila went very white. Pat hurriedly put on another record. Janet took up her book again, still angry, but rather ashamed. If Sheila had said nothing more, the whole thing might have blown over. But after a while Sheila raised her voice and addressed Janet.

"I'm sure that if my people knew that I had to put up with girls like *you*, Janet, they would never have sent me to St. Clare's," she began. "You've no manners at all, you . . ."

"Manners! *You* talk about manners!" raged Janet, flinging down her book again. "Good heavens! What about your own manners, I should like to know! You can begin to talk about other people's when you know how to wash your neck and brush your hair, and how to eat decently! And then you pretend you are too grand for us! Huh!"

Janet stamped out of the room. Sheila sat perfectly still, very pale. The twins glanced at her, and Pat put on yet another record, setting it at "Loud". What an awful quarrel!

After a while Sheila went out of the room. Pat switched off the gramophone. "Didn't she look awful?" she said to Isabel. "I wish Janet hadn't said all that. "It's true it's what we've all thought, and perhaps said to one another in joke – but its rather awful to blurt it all out like that."

"Well, it's partly Sheila's own silly fault," said Hilary. "If she wouldn't swank as she does, and try to make out she's someone marvellous, we wouldn't notice so easily the stupid things she does and says. I mean to say – if people swank about five different bathrooms, one pink, one blue, one green, one yellow and one mauve, and then don't trouble to wash their necks, you do notice it rather!"

"Yes – she's funny about her bathrooms!" said Isabel. "She's funny altogether. She's the only girl in the form that I really and truly don't know at all. I mean, I don't know if she's generous or mean, kind or unkind, honest or dishonest, truthful or untruthful, jolly or serious – because she's always pretending about herself – putting on airs and graces, swanking, being somebody that she isn't. She might be quite nice, for all we know!"

"I shouldn't think so," said Hilary, who was heartily tired of Sheila and her nonsense. "Honestly, I think she's batty."

Sheila didn't come in for tea, but nobody missed her. When she didn't attend evening preparation in the form room, Miss Roberts sent Pat to find her. Pat hunted all over the place, and at last came across Sheila sitting in a deserted and cold little music room, all by herself.

"Sheila! What in the world are you doing?" asked Pat. "Have you forgotten it's prep. tonight?"

Sheila sat still and said nothing. Pat looked at her

closely. She looked ill.

"Don't you feel well?" asked Pat. "I'll take you to Matron if you like. What's up, Sheila old girl?"

"Nothing," said Sheila.

"Well, what are you sitting here for, all in the cold?" asked Pat. "Don't be an idiot. If you're not ill, come along to prep. Miss Roberts is getting all hot and bothered about you."

"I'm not coming," said Sheila. "I can't face you all again, after what Janet said."

"Well, really! Fancy taking any notice of Janet!" said Pat, feeling worried. "You know how she loses her temper with all of us, and says things she doesn't mean. She's forgotten all about it by now. Come along!"

"She didn't say things she didn't mean. That's the whole point," said Sheila, still in the same quiet, rather queer voice. "She said things she *did* mean! Oh, I hate her!"

"You can't hate old Janet!" said Pat. "She's dreadfully quick-tempered and impatient, but she's very kind too. She wouldn't *really* hurt you, Sheila. Look here — I'm sure you're not well. Come with me to Matron. Perhaps you've got a temperature."

"Leave me alone," said Sheila, obstinately. So in despair Pat left her, feeling very worried. What a pity Janet had flared out like that, and said those really dreadful things! Pat knew how she would feel if anyone sneered at her in that way in front of every one. She wondered what to do. What should she tell Miss Roberts?

On her way back to the form room she passed the head-girl's study. The door was a little open and Pat could just see Winifred James bent over a book. She hesitated outside, as a thought came into her head.

She couldn't tell Miss Roberts about the awful quarrel. But could she tell Winifred? Something had got to be done about Sheila, and she simply didn't know what! She knocked at Winifred's door.

"Come in!" said the head-girl, and raised her serious face as Pat came in.

"Hallo! Is there anything the matter?" asked Winifred. "Oughtn't you to be at prep?"

"Yes, I ought," said Pat. "But Miss Roberts sent me to find somebody. And I'm rather worried about this girl, Winifred, but I can't possibly tell Miss Roberts, so can I tell you?"

"Of course," said Winifred, "so long as it isn't just telling tales, Patricia."

"Of course it's not, Winifred!" said Pat. "I would never tell tales. But I suddenly remembered that you and this girl come from the same town, so I thought maybe you could help a bit."

"This is very mysterious," said Winifred. "What's it all about?"

Then Pat explained about the quarrel, and told the head-girl all that had happened. "And Sheila looks so funny and so ill," she said. "I'm afraid it's something worse than just a silly quarrel."

Winifred listened in silence. "I'm glad you came to me," she said. "It so happens I'm the only person that can help a little, because I know Sheila's history. You are a sensible person, Pat, so I shall tell you a little. And perhaps between us we can help Sheila."

"I hope we can," said Pat. "I don't like her, Winifred – in fact, I hardly know her at all because she's always hidden behind conceit and swank, if you know what I mean. But she's awfully unhappy and I hate to see that."

"Sheila's parents were once very poor," said Winifred. "Her mother was the daughter of our gardener. Her father kept a kind of village stores. He made a great deal of money, an enormous fortune, in fact, so they rose tremendously in the world. Now they have a wonderful house, almost a mansion, goodness knows how many servants and cars – and they sent Sheila to the best schools possible because they wanted their daughter to be a lady."

"Oh," said Pat, suddenly understanding a lot of things. "So that's why poor Sheila is always swanking and being haughty and arrogant, and showing off – because she's afraid we'll not want to be friends with her. She's afraid we might sneer at her."

"Yes – her stupid haughtiness is just a sort of smoke-screen to hide the plain, ordinary, rather frightened person she is underneath," said Winifred. "And now you see what as happened. Janet has blown away the smoke-screen and pointed out to every one just those things that Sheila is always trying to hide – the manners and speech she learnt when she was very small."

"But how awfully silly of Sheila to pretend like that!" said Pat. "If she'd told us honestly that her people had made a lot of money, and how pleased she was to be able to come to St. Clare's, and all that, we'd have understood and liked her for it. But all that silly conceit and pretence! Honestly, Winifred, it was awful."

"When people feel that they are not so clever, so good or so well-born as others, they often behave like that, to hide their feelings of inferiority," said Winifred, sounding rather learned to Pat. "Be sorry for them and help them."

"Well – how can I help Sheila?" asked Pat. "I really don't see how I can."

"I'll go to her myself," said Winifred, getting up. "All I want *you* to do – and Isabel too – is to be extra nice to her for a week or two, and not to laugh at her or point out anything that might hurt her. Now that Janet has dragged away the wall Sheila set up round herself, and shown what a poor thing there is behind it, she will want a little friendship and understanding. If she's got any common sense she'll drop her airs and graces after this, and you'll have a chance of finding out what the real Sheila is like. But do give her a chance, won't you?"

"Of course I will," said Pat. "Thanks awfully, Winifred. I'll go back to prep. now."

What Winifred said to Sheila the twins never knew. The head-girl was wise beyond her years, and handled the shocked and distressed girl with understanding and gentleness. Sheila appeared in the common room that night, pale and nervous, and would not meet any one's eyes. But Pat came to her rescue at once.

"Sheila! You're just the person I wanted! *Please* tell me where I've gone wrong in this jumper I'm knitting. You're so clever at following patterns and I get all muddled. Look – did I go wrong there – or was it here?"

Sheila gladly went to Pat's side, and was soon showing her how to put the wrong stitch right. When that was done, Isabel called to her. "Hi, Sheila – will you lend me your paints? I can't imagine what's happened to mine."

"Yes, of course," said Sheila, and went to fetch her paints. Janet looked up as soon as she was out of the room.

"Why all this sudden friendship for our haughty Sheila?" she asked.

"To make up a bit for the beastly things you said to her," said Pat. "Give her a chance, Janet. You've hit her hard on her tenderest places, and taken all the stuffing out of her."

"Good thing too," said Janet, gruffly. "She needed it."

"Well, she's had it, so now give her a chance," said Pat. "Don't be small, Janet."

"I'm not," said Janet. "I'm jolly sorry for what I said now, though you may not think it. All right – I'll do my bit. But I'm not going to say I'm sorry. If I do it'll get her all hot and bothered again. But I don't mind *showing* I'm sorry."

"Better still," said Isabel. "Look out – here she comes!"

Sheila came in with the paints. "Thanks," said Isabel. "Golly, what a lovely box!"

Usually Sheila would have said at once what the box had cost, and would have boasted about it. But she said nothing. Janet glanced at her and saw that she was still pale. Janet was kind-hearted and generous, although her tongue could be sharp and bitter, and her temper was hot. She got down a tin of toffees from her shelf and handed them round. Sheila expected to be missed out and looked away.

"Toffee for you, Sheila, old girl?" said Janet, in her clear, pleasant voice. Sheila looked at Janet and hesitated. She still felt sore and angry with her. But Janet's brown eyes were kind and soft, and Sheila knew that she was trying to make peace. She swallowed her feelings, and put out her hand to take a toffee.

"Thanks, Janet," she said, in rather a shaky voice. Then all the girls plunged into a discussion of the play they were going to prepare for Christmas, and in the interest of it all Sheila forgot the quarrel, sucked her toffee, and grew happier.

She thought hard when she went to bed that night. She shouldn't have boasted and bragged – but she had only done it because she knew she wasn't as good as the others and she wanted to hide it. And all the time the girls had seen her weak spots, and must have laughed at her boasting. Well – if only they would be friendly towards her and not sneer at her, she would try not to mind. She was not a brave girl, and not a very sensible one – but that night she was brave enough and sensible enough to see that money and servants and cars didn't matter at all. It was the person underneath that mattered.

"And now I'll do what Winifred said I must do – show the girls the person I am underneath," thought poor Sheila, turning over in bed. "I don't think I'm much of a person really – but anyway, I'll be better than that awful conceited creature I've pretended to be for a year!"

And that was the end of Sheila's haughty and boastful manner. The other girls followed the example of Janet and the twins, and were friendly to Sheila, and gave her a chance. She took the chance, and although, as she had feared, she wasn't much of a person at first, nevertheless the rather mouse-like gentle Sheila was much nicer than the girl she had been before. As time went on, she would become somebody real, and then as Pat said, she would be worth having for a friend.

"I shall always give people a chance now," Pat said to Isabel. "Look at Kathleen – what a brick she is! And Sheila's so different, already."

"Well," said Janet, who overheard, "I should jolly well think you *would* give people a chance! Didn't we all give *you* two a chance! My goodness, you were pretty unbearable when you came, I can tell you. But you're not so bad now. In fact, you're quite passable!"

Pat and Isabel picked up cushions and rushed at the quick-tongued Janet. With squeals and shrieks she tried to get away, but they pummelled her unmercifully.

"We shan't give *you* a chance, you wretch!" giggled Isabel. "You don't deserve one! Ow, stop pinching, you brute."

"Well, get off my middle then," panted Janet. "Wait till *I* get hold of a cushion!"

But they didn't wait! They tore off to gym. with Janet after them, bumping into half a dozen girls on the way.

"Those first-form kids!" said Tessie, in disgust. "Honestly, they ought to be in a kindergarten, they way they behave!"

114

The Twins pummelled Janet with the cushions

Only four weeks remained of the winter term. The girls were busy with plays, songs and sketches, ready for the end of the term. The first form were doing a historical play with Miss Kennedy and thoroughly enjoying themselves.

Miss Kennedy had written the play herself with the girls all helping where they could. Miss Ross, the sewing mistress, was helping with the costumes. It was great fun.

"You know, old Kenny is a good sort," said Pat, who was busily learning her part for the play. "It's funny – I hardly ever think of playing about in her lesson now. I suppose it's because we're all so interested in the play."

"Well, I wish I was as interested in our French play!" groaned Doris, whose French accent drove Mam'zelle to despair. "I simply can NOT roll my *r's* in my throat like the rest of you. R-r-r-r-r-r-r-r!"

Every one laughed at Doris's funny efforts to say the letter *r* in the French way. Doris had no ear for either music or languages, and was the despair of both the music mistress and Mam'zelle. But she was a wonderful dancer, and her sense of humour sent the class into fits of laughter half a dozen times a day.

It was fun preparing for the Christmas concert. All the different forms were doing something, and there were squabbles over using the gym. for rehearsals. Miss Thomas, the gym. mistress, complained that the gym. was used for everything else but its proper purpose these days!

Lessons went on as usual, of course, and Miss Roberts refused to allow the Christmas preparations to make any difference at all to the work her form did for her. She was very cross with Pat when she found that she was secretly learning her part in the play, when she should have been learning a list of grammar rules.

Pat had copied out her words, and had neatly fitted them into her grammar book. She had a good part in the play and was very anxious to be word-perfect for the rehearsal that afternoon.

"I think, Pat, that you must have got the wrong page in your grammar book," said Miss Roberts, suddenly. "Bring it to me."

Pat went red. She got up with her book. She dropped it purposely on the floor so that it shut, and then picked it up, hoping that Miss Roberts would not notice the words of the play inside. But Miss Roberts did, of course. Her sharp eyes missed nothing!

"I thought so," she said, dryly, taking out the neatly-copied play-words. "When is the rehearsal?"

"This afternoon, Miss Roberts," said Pat.

"Well, you will learn your grammar rules instead of going to the rehearsal," said Miss Roberts. "That seems quite fair to me, and I hope it does to you. If you learn your part in the play during grammar time, then it seems just that you should learn your grammar rules in rehearsal time."

Pat looked up in dismay. "Oh, Miss Roberts! Please don't make me miss rehearsal. I've got an important part in the play, you know."

"Yes, and next year this form has important exams. to take," said Miss Roberts. "Well, I'll give you one more chance, Pat. No more of this, please! Learn those rules now and say them to me at the end of the morning. If they are correct, I'll let you off. Go back to your seat!"

Pat went to the rehearsal, of course! It was just no

good at all trying to play any tricks in Miss Roberts' class, and she had had to learn her grammar in break in order to get it perfect for Miss Roberts by the end of the morning.

But every one liked the form-mistress. She was strict, could be very severe and sarcastic, but she was always perfectly just, and never went back on what she said or promised. Mam'zelle was not always just, but she was so goodhearted that very few of the girls really disliked her.

What with working up for the end of term exams., and the concert, the girls had very little time to themselves, but they enjoyed every minute. Doris was to dance a solo dance that she had created herself. Vera was to play the piano, at which she was extremely good. Five of the girls were in the French play, and most of them in the history play. Everybody was in something.

Except one person! Sheila was in nothing! This happened quite by accident. At first Mam'zelle had said she was to be Monsieur Toc-Toc in the play, so Miss Kennedy didn't put her in the history play – and then Mam'zelle changed her mind and put Joan into the French play instead. So Sheila was in neither, and as she didn't play the piano or the violin, could not recite at all, and was no good at dancing, she felt very left-out.

She said nothing. At first nobody noticed that she wasn't going to be in anything, because it had all happened accidentally. Then Isabel noticed that Sheila was looking mopey and asked her why.

"What's up? Had bad news from home or something?"

"Oh, no," said Sheila. "Nothing's wrong."

Isabel said no more but watched Sheila for a few days. She soon noticed that she was not in either of the plays and was not doing anything by herself either.

"I say! I believe you're miserable because you're not

118

in the concert!" said Isabel. "I thought you were going to be in the French play."

"I was," said Sheila, uncomfortably. "But then Mam-'zelle chose some one else. I'm not in anything, and every one will notice it, Isabel. I do so hate being left out."

"Well, it wasn't done on purpose, silly," said Isabel, laughing.

"I feel as if it was," said Sheila. "I know I'm not much good at anything, but it doesn't make it any better when I'm not even given the *chance* to do anything."

"Oh, don't be an idiot!" said Isabel. Sheila looked obstinate. Like many weak people she could be really pig-headed.

"Well, I'm fed up!" she said. "I shan't go to the rehearsal or anything. I'll just go off by myself."

"Well, anyway, you might at least take an interest in what the form is doing, even if you're not doing anything yourself!" cried Isabel, indignantly. "That's mean and stupid."

"I'll be mean and stupid then," said Sheila, almost in tears, and she went off by herself.

Isabel told Pat. "Oh blow!" said Pat. "Just as we were getting Sheila to be sensible too, and giving her a chance. Don't let's bother about her! If she wants to feel she's left out and slighted when she isn't, let her!"

Janet came up and listened to the tale. She had been very good to Sheila the last week or two, for she had really felt very guilty over her loss of temper. She looked thoughtful now. "No – don't let's undo the good work we've been trying to do!" she said. "Let's think of something. I know once I was left out of a match when I badly wanted to be in it, and although I'm not such a silly as Sheila, still I did feel pretty awful. I remember thinking that the whole school would be whispering about me, wondering what I had done to be out of the match!"

The twins laughed. Janet was so sensible and jolly that they couldn't imagine her worrying about a thing like that.

"It's all very well to laugh," said Janet. "You are twins and have always got each other to back up and laugh over things with – but when you're a naturally lonely person like Sheila, it's different. Little things get awfully big."

"You *are* sticking up for Sheila all of a sudden," said Pat, in surprise.

"No, I'm not. All I say is – don't let's spoil what we've been trying to *do*," said Janet, impatiently.

"Oh, well – you think of something then," said Isabel. "I can't!"

The twins went off. Janet sat down and began to think. She was impatient and impulsive, but once she had set her hand to anything she wouldn't give up. Sheila wanted help again, and Janet was going to give it.

"Gosh! I've got it!" said Janet to herself. "We'll make her prompter, of course! We need some one at rehearsals with the book, ready to prompt any of us who forgets. And my goodness, I forget my words all right! I'll go and ask Sheila if she'll be prompter at rehearsals and on the concert night too."

She went off to find Sheila. It was some time before she found her, and then at last she ran her to earth in the art room, tidying out the cupboards.

"I say, Sheila! Will you do something for us?" cried Janet. "Will you be prompter for the play? We get into an awful muddle trying to prompt each other, and it would be an awful help to have some one with the book, who will follow the words and help when we go wrong."

"I wouldn't be any good at that," said Sheila, rather sullenly.

"Oh, yes, you would, idiot!" said Janet. "It *would* be such a help, Sheila. Please do. Some of us are sure to be nervous on the concert night too, and it would be nice to know you were at the side, ready to prompt us with the words."

"All right," said Sheila, rather ungraciously. She had felt that if she wasn't in the plays, she jolly well wouldn't help at all. But that was small and mean – and Sheila was doing her best not to be that.

So she became prompter, and attended all the rehearsals with the book of words. She soon began to enjoy it all, and loved the play. She did nothing but stand or sit with the book, prompting those who forgot, whilst the others had the fun of acting. But she didn't grumble or complain, and the twins secretly thought she was behaving rather well.

"Good for Janet to have thought of that," said Pat.

"Yes – she thought Sheila was going to refuse," said Isabel. "I'm not at all sure *I* wouldn't have said no, if it had been me!"

"I shouldn't have let you!" said Pat.

Two weeks before the end of the term an accident happened. Vera, a very quiet girl in the first form, fell during gym. and broke her arm. She broke it just by the wrist and had to be taken off to hospital to have it X-rayed. It was set in plaster, and her parents decided that as it was so near the end of the term, she might as well go home, instead of staying the last two weeks.

"It's her right arm, so she won't be able to write at all," said her mother to Miss Theobald. "It would be just as well for her to be quiet at home."

So poor Vera said good-bye and went, promising to be back the next term with her arm mended again! And then there was consternation in the class, because Vera had an important part in the play!

"Golly! What's to be done?" said Pat, in dismay.

"No one else can possibly learn all the words in time. Vera had such a big part."

Every one stared round in despair. Those who were not in the play felt perfectly certain that they could not possibly learn the big part in so short a time. And then Janet spoke.

"There's some one who *does* know all the words!" she cried. "Sheila, you do! You've been prompting us at every rehearsal, and you know every part! You're the only one who's been following the words page by page in the book. Can't *you* take Vera's part?"

Sheila went bright red. All the girls looked at her expectantly.

"Go on – say you will," said Pat. "You can do it just as well as Vera!"

"I should love to," said Sheila. "I'm sure I could do it! I know every word! Well – I know every word of every part now, of course – but I'd just love to do Vera's part. I like it best of all."

"Good!" cried Pat. "That's settled then. We'll get some one else to be prompter and you must be in the play."

"So at the next rehearsal Sheila was not prompter, but took one of the most important parts. She was quite word-perfect, and because she had so often watched Vera doing the part, she was able to act it very well.

Every one was pleased. They had all known that Sheila was hurt because she had been left out of everything by accident, and had admired her for taking on the rather dull job of prompter – and now that she had had such an unexpected reward the whole form was delighted.

But nobody was more delighted than Sheila herself. She was really thrilled with her good luck. She went about with a smiling face, and was so unexpectedly jolly that the class could hardly believe it was Sheila.

But Sheila did not forget to write and tell Vera how sorry she was to hear about her accident. She remembered some one else's disappointment in the middle of her own pleasure. Yes – Sheila was well on the way to becoming somebody now!

Kathleen Has A Secret

One afternoon, when Pat, Isabel and Kathleen were coming back from the town across the fields, they heard a whining noise from the hedge.

"That's a dog!" said Kathleen at once, and she ran to see. The others followed – and there, in the ditch, they saw a half-grown rough-haired terrier, its chest and face bleeding.

"It's been shot!" cried Kathleen indignantly. "Look at all the pellets in its poor legs! Oh! It's that hateful farmer who lives over the hill. He always swears he'll shoot any dog that goes wandering in his fields."

"But why?" asked Pat, in surprise. "Dogs go all over the fields."

"Yes – but sheep are in these fields, and soon the lambs will be born," said Kathleen. "Dogs chase sheep, you know, and frighten them."

"Well, this poor animal has been shot," said Pat. "What are we going to do with it?"

"I'm going to take it back to school with me and look after it," said Kathleen. She was quite crazy over animals. The twins looked at her in astonishment.

"You won't be able to keep him," said Pat. "And anyway, you ought to ring up the police and report him. Suppose his owner is looking for him?"

"Well, I'll ring up and see if any one has been asking

for him," said Kathleen. "But if you think I'm going to leave a dog bleeding all by itself out in the fields, you're jolly well mistaken!"

"All right, all right!" said Isabel. "But how are you going to take him home? He'll cover you with blood."

"As if I care about that!" said Kathleen, picking the dog up very gently. He whined again, but snuggled down into the girl's arms, knowing quite well that they were kind and friendly.

They walked back to school with the dog. They debated where to put him. No girl was allowed to keep a dog, and if he were discovered he would certainly be sent off. And Kathleen was quite determined that she was going to nurse him till he was better!

"Could we keep him in the bicycle shed?" asked Pat.

"Oh, no. He would be much too cold," said Kathleen, standing behind the bushes with the dog in her arms, pondering how to get him into school without being seen. "Wait a minute – let's think."

They all thought. Then Pat gave an exclamation. "I know! What about that little box-room near the hot tank upstairs in the attics? He'd be warm there, and right away from every one. Nobody ever goes there."

"And we're not supposed to either," said Isabel. "Dash! We always seem to be doing things we oughtn't to do."

"Well, this is for the dog's sake," said Kathleen. "I'm willing to do anything. Poor darling! Don't whine like that. I promise I'll make you better soon."

Janet came round the corner and saw the three of them standing by the bushes. "Hallo!" she said. "What's up? What have you got there? A dog! Goodness gracious, what's wrong with him?"

"He's been shot," said Kathleen. "We're going to keep him in the boxroom upstairs in the attics till he's better. Are you going down to the town, Janet? Well,

They debated where to put the dog

be a sport and ask at the police station if anyone has reported a lost dog. If they have, ask for their name and address, and I'll tell them I've got him safely."

"All right," said Janet. "But look out that he doesn't make a noise or you'll get into trouble. You're quite batty over animals, Kathleen! Good-bye!"

Janet rushed off to get her bicycle. Kathleen turned to the twins. "You go and see that the coast is clear," she said. "And let's think what to have for a bed for him."

"There's an old wooden box in the gardener's shed," said Isabel, eagerly. "That would do nicely. I'll get it."

She ran to get it. Pat went indoors to see if it was safe for Kathleen to take the dog in. She whistled a little tune, and Kathleen ran in with the dog. The two of them scurried up the stairs without meeting any one – but round the corner of the corridor they could hear footsteps coming and the loud voice of Mam'zelle, talking to Miss Jenks.

"Oh, crumbs!" groaned Kathleen, and she turned to go down the stairs again. But some one was now coming up. Pat opened the door of a big broom cupboard and pushed Kathleen and the dog into it. She shut the door, and then dropped on one knee, pretending to do up her shoe. Just as Mam'zelle and Miss Jenks passed her, the dog in the cupboard gave a whine. Mam'zelle looked round in surprise.

"*Tiens!* Why do you whine like a dog?" she asked Pat, and passed on, thinking that girls were indeed funny creatures. Pat giggled, and opened the door when the two mistresses had gone by.

"Did you hear what Mam'zelle said?" she asked. "Come on – it's all right now. We can get up the attic stairs in a trice!"

They went up to the top of the school. The attics were just under the roof, and the boxrooms were a peculiar shape, being small, with slanting roofs, and almost impossible to stand up in. Here were kept the trunks and cases belonging to the girls. The boxrooms were only visited twice a term – once when the trunks were put there, and once when they were brought down to be packed.

After a moment Isabel came up with the box and an old rug she had found in the locker downstairs in the gym. The girls chose the little boxroom next to the hot tanks. It was warm and cosy. They set the wooden box down in a corner and tucked the old rug into it. It made a very cosy bed.

Then Kathleen set to work to bathe the dog's wounds. It took a long time, and the dog lay patiently till it was finished, licking Kathleen's careful hands as she bathed him.

"You're awfully good with animals," said Pat, watching her. "And doesn't he love you?"

"I'm going to be a vet when I'm grown up," said Kathleen. "There you are, my beauty. You're all right now. Don't lick off that ointment more than you can help! Lie quietly here now, and you'll soon be all right again! I'll bring you some water and some food."

The bell went for prep. and the three girls hurried downstairs, carefully closing the boxroom door behind them. They met Janet as they went into the classroom.

"I asked at the police station," whispered Janet. "But they said nobody had reported a dog. I had to tell them what he was like and they wanted your name and address."

"Gracious! What an idiot you are!" whispered back Kathleen, as she took her seat. "Whatever will Miss Theobald say if the police ring up the school and ask for me! Really, Janet!"

"Well, I *had* to give it!" whispered Janet. "You can't say no to the police, can you? Anyway, I don't expect the dog will be reported, so don't worry!"

But Kathleen did worry. When she heard the telephone bell ringing that evening she was quite sure that it was the police ringing up the Head Mistress. But it wasn't. The girls breathed with relief when they heard that it was a message for Miss Roberts.

The dog was given water and food. He lay quite quietly in his basket and was as good as gold. "He ought to have a run before we go to bed," said Kathleen, anxiously. "How are we to manage it?"

"Let's bundle him up in a heap of the clothes we are using for the play," said Pat. "If anyone meets us they will think we are just taking a pile of clothes for rehearsal. I'll get some!"

So, five minutes before bedtime the girls crept up the attic stairs with a heap of clothes. The surprised dog was carefully tucked up in them, with just his nose showing so that he could breathe.

Then Kathleen carried him downstairs, whispering to him so that he would lie quiet. He did not want to be quiet at all, and struggled violently, but luckily the girls met nobody except Matron. She was in a hurry, and hardly glanced at them.

"You won't be in time for bed if you aren't quick!" she called. The girls giggled, and went out into the garden by a little-used door. They set the dog free in a tiny yard where the gardeners chopped firewood and logs, and he limped about joyfully. Then they packed him up in the pile of clothes again, and scurried indoors.

This time they were not so lucky. They met Belinda Towers! She stopped and glared at them.

"Don't you know that your bed-time bell has gone? What are you doing wandering about here? And what on earth is that in those clothes?"

The dog struggled to get out and its head came out with a jerk. "Oh, we've been trying so hard not to let any one see him!" said Kathleen, almost in tears. "Belinda, he's been shot, he's . . ."

"Don't tell me anything about him and I shan't know," said Belinda, who was very fond of animals too. "Go on – take that pile of clothes away – and go to your dormitory quickly."

"Good old Belinda!" said Pat, as the three of them ran up the stairs to the boxroom. "Isn't she a sport? Talk about Nelson turning the blind eye – she turned a blind eye on our dog all right! Do hurry, Kath. We really shall get into a row if we're much longer!"

They tucked the dog up again in his basket. He licked their hands and wuffed a very small bark. "Isn't he clever?" cried Kathleen, in delight. "He even knows he must whisper a bark."

"Well, it was a pretty loud whisper," said Pat. "Come on. Let's go down and hope that Hilary won't say a word. It's about the first time we've been late, anyway. I hope the dog doesn't bark the place down in the night!"

"Of course he won't!" said Kathleen, shutting the boxroom door carefully. "He'll sleep all night – and in the morning, very early, I'll take him for a run again."

They tore down to their dormitory, to find Hilary getting most exasperated with them. "Where *have* you been?" she demanded. "You know it's my job to see you're here on time at nine o'clock. It's too bad of you."

"We've been putting a dog to bed," whispered Kathleen. Hilary stared in surprise.

"*What* did you say?" she asked. "Putting *what* to bed?"

"Shall I tell every one?" said Kathleen to the twins. They nodded. It was lovely to have a secret – but it was great fun to surprise every one and tell it!

So Kathleen explained about the hurt dog, and every one listened in amazement. "Fancy taking a dog to the boxroom!" cried Doris. "Well, I'd never dare to do that! Suppose Matron went up there! She'd soon find him!"

"Well, we shall only keep him for a day or two till he's quite better," said Kathleen. "Then we'll have found out where he belongs to and can take him back."

But it wasn't quite as easy as all that!

The Secret Is Out!

The dog made no noise at all in the night. Kathleen managed to wake very early, and creep up to the box-room to take him for a run in the little wood-yard. He completely refused to be taken down all wrapped up again, so Kathleen had to put a bit of string round his neck and lead him down the stairs. He made rather a noise flopping down, but nobody came to see what was the matter.

It was marvellous the way his legs and chest and face had healed during the night. Kathleen was very pleased. The dog fawned round her legs in the yard, and tried to jump up to lick her hand. The girl thought he was a marvellous dog, and hoped against hope that no one would claim him.

"If only I could keep him until the end of term, and then take him home!" she thought. "Wouldn't it be lovely!"

She took him back to the boxroom again. This time he didn't want her to leave him, and after she had shut the door and gone back to the dormitory she felt sure she could hear him whining and scraping against the door.

The first-form's classroom was just underneath the boxrooms. The room where the dog was was not ex-actly overhead but more to the right. Kathleen listened anxiously to see if he was making any noise during school time. Her sharp ears heard the patter of feet and small whines, but Miss Roberts apparently heard nothing.

When Mam'zelle came to take a French lesson, however, she heard the dog quite plainly! Her ears were exceedingly keen. The first time that the dog whined, she looked up in surprise.

"What can that noise be?" she said.

"What noise, Mam'zelle?" asked Isabel, with an innocent face.

"The noise of a dog!" said Mam'zelle, impatiently. "The whine, the bark! Is it possible that you have not heard it, Isabel!"

All the class pretended to listen hard. Then the girls shook their heads.

"You must be mistaken, Mam'zelle," said Doris, gravely.

"There surely isn't a dog in the school," said Joan. "Only the kitchen cats."

Mam'zelle was really most astonished to think that she was the only one who heard the strange noises.

"Ah, it must be something wrong with my ears, then," she said, and she shook her big head vigorously. "I will get the doctor to syringe them for me. I cannot have dogs barking and whining in my head."

The class, already in a state of giggle, was glad to burst into laughter at this. Mam'zelle rapped on the desk.

"Enough! I made no joke! Take down *dictée*, please."

The class went on with its work. The dog in the box-room explored the place thoroughly, and, judging by the noise, tried a good deal of scratching at the door and the walls. Mam'zelle looked extremely puzzled once or twice, and glanced at the girls to see if they too had noticed the noises – but one and all went serenely

131

on with their work, and appeared to hear nothing – so Mam'zelle pressed her ears thoughtfully, and made up her mind to see the doctor that very same day.

The twins and Kathleen spent most of their free time in the boxroom with the dog. It was always so pleased to see them, and they all grew very fond of it indeed. The only exasperating thing was that when they left it, it *would* bark and whine after them, and try to scratch the door open. They were always afraid that somebody would hear it then.

But two days went by safely, and it was not discovered. The girls fed it, gave it water, and took it down secretly for runs in the woodyard. Kathleen really adored the little creature, and indeed it was a very intelligent and affectionate animal.

"As nobody has claimed to be its owner, I really think I might keep it for myself, don't you?" asked Kathleen, anxiously, as she and the twins stroked the dog up in the boxroom one free half-hour. "I do love him so. He really is a darling. I couldn't bear to take him to the police-station now and leave him there. You know, if nobody claimed him at all the police would have him put to sleep."

"Well, you keep him then," said Pat. "There isn't much longer till the end of the term. But you'll have to move him out of here when the maids come up to get down our boxes for us. That's very soon. I don't see what you're going to do, really I don't!"

However, the twins and Kathleen did not need to bother about what was going to happen because the dog soon decided things for himself.

One morning, about four days after he had been found, he lay down in a bit of wintry sunshine that came slanting through the attic window. It made him feel restless and he jumped up and prowled round. He came to the door and stood sniffing at it. Then he began to jump at the handle.

After a while he managed, quite by chance, to jerk the catch back – and the door opened! The dog was delighted. He pushed it wide open with his nose and trotted down the attic stairs.

Now all might still have been well if one of the school cats had not been lying fast asleep on a mat underneath one of the corridor radiators. The dog sniffed the cat-smell, and trotted up in delight. What! A cat! And what was more, a cat asleep!

With a loud wuff the dog leapt on the cat in play. It was only a puppy and would not really have hurt it – but the cat was in a most terrible fright. It leapt up, gave an anguished yowl, and fled down the corridor, its tail straight up in the air. The dog gave chase at once, prancing along on all four puppy-legs! And that was how Miss Theobald met the dog.

She was going along to one of the classrooms when first the cat and then the dog shot round her legs. She turned in amazement. Cats there were in the school, because of mice – but where in the world did a dog suddenly appear from?

The cat leapt out of a window. The dog paused, surprised that the cat had disappeared so suddenly. Then he decided to go and find Kathleen. He thought he had smelt her somewhere along the passage. So off he trotted again, and soon came to the first-form class-room. He stood up on his hind legs and whined and scratched.

Mam'zelle was once again giving a French lesson, and the whole class was busy correcting its French prep., and writing out various mistakes. When the dog jumped up at the door and whined, Mam'zelle leapt to her feet.

"*Tiens!* This time it is not my ears! It is in truth a

dog!" She marched to the door and opened it. In ran the dog, his tail wagging nineteen to the dozen, and went straight to Kathleen. How all the class stared!

And after him came Miss Theobald, determined to unravel the mystery of the dog! She looked into the classroom and saw Mam'zelle stamping up and down, and Kathleen doing her best to quiet the excited dog!

"What is all this disturbance?" asked Miss Theobald, in her quiet, serious voice. Mam'zelle turned to her at once, her hands wagging above her shoulders as she poured out how she had heard a dog some days ago, and how he had come to the door and scratched.

"I think perhaps Kathleen knows more about him than any one," said Miss Theobald, noticing how the animal fawned on the girl, and how she stroked and patted him. "Kathleen, come with me, and perhaps you can give me an explanation."

Kathleen, rather pale, stood up. She followed the Head to her room, the dog trotting amiably at her heels. Miss Theobald made her sit down.

"I didn't mean to do any wrong," said Kathleen, beginning her tale "But he was so hurt, Miss Theobald, and I do so much love dogs, and I've never had any pet of my own, and . . ."

"Begin at the beginning," said the Head. So Kathleen told the whole story, and Miss Theobald listened. At the end she reached for the telephone and took off the receiver. She asked for the police station. Kathleen's heart stood still! Whatever was the Head going to say!

Miss Theobald enquired if any dog had been reported missing. Apparently none had. Then she asked what would happen if a dog was kept, that had been found hurt. "It had no collar when it was found," she explained.

After a while she put down the receiver and turned to Kathleen, who now had the dog on her knee.

"I can't imagine how you have kept the dog hidden all this time," she said, "and I am not going to enquire. I know you are fond of animals. Well, apparently there is no reason why you should not keep the dog for yourself, if no one claims it within a certain time. So I propose to let you keep it until you return home for the holidays, and if your aunt will let you have it, you can take it back. But it must be kept in the stables, Kathleen. For once in a way I will relax the rule that says no pet must be kept, and let you have the dog until the holidays."

If Kathleen had not been in such awe of the Head she would certainly have flung her arms round her neck! As it was she could hardly swallow a lump that suddenly appeared in her throat, which made it very difficult for her to say anything. But she managed to stammer out her thanks. The dog was not in awe of Miss Theobald, however – and he went to her and licked her hands solemnly, for all the world as if he knew what had been said!

"Take him to the stables now, and get one of the men to find a good place for him," said Miss Theobald. "And next time you want to do anything peculiar, Kathleen, come and ask either me or Miss Roberts first! It really would save quite a lot of trouble!"

Kathleen hurried off, her eyes shining. The dog trotted after her. Before she went to the stables the girl ran back to her classroom and burst in, her cheeks flushed and her eyes sparkling.

"I say!" she cried. "I'm to keep the dog. I'm to take him home if my aunt . . ."

"Kathleen! I will not have my class interrupted in this scandalous way!" cried Mam'zelle, rising in wrath from her desk. Kathleen took one look at her and disappeared. She went to the stables and found one of the gardeners. He soon gave the dog a place, and Kathleen left him, happy in the thought that now she could come and take him for a walk whenever she wanted to.

On her way back to her form she met Belinda Towers, off for a practice in the lacrosse field. "Belinda!" she cried. "The dog escaped and came to me in the classroom! And he chased a cat and Miss Theobald saw him and came after him – and she's letting me keep him!"

"Good for you!" said Belinda. "Now buzz off back to your form. You first-form kids always seem to be doing something extraordinary!"

Kathleen buzzed off. She went very, very quietly back to the French lesson and sat down. Mam'zelle still had a lot to say, but the words rolled off Kathleen's head like water off a duck's back. She sat and dreamed of the dog who was really to be her very own.

"And if you do not pay more attention to me I will give you a three-page essay to write about dogs in French!" she suddenly heard Mam'zelle say, and pulled herself together. The whole class was grinning at her. Mam'zelle was glaring, half-angry, half-amused, for the girl had really not heard a word until then.

Kathleen didn't at all want to write a three-page essay in French. Good gracious! She wouldn't be able to take the dog for a walk. So for the next twenty minutes she worked harder than any one in the class, and Mam'zelle said no more!

And during the half-hour between morning school and dinner, four girls crowded round an excited dog and quarrelled as to what name he should be given!

"I'm his owner and I'm going to choose!" said Kathleen, firmly. "His name is Binks. I don't know why – but he looks like a Binks to me."

So Binks he was, and Binks he remained till the last day of term came and he went home with Kathleen.

What a time he had till then, with dozens of girls clamouring to take him for walks, and bringing him so many things to eat that he grew as fat as a barrel! Even the mistresses loved him and gave him a pat when they met him out with Kathleen.

All but Mam'zelle, who thought that school was no place for dogs! "He is abominable!" she said, whenever she saw him. "That dog! How he disturbed my class!" But there was a twinkle in her eye, so nobody took her seriously!

A Shock For Isabel

Exams. began. The twins were very anxious to do well in them, for they badly wanted to be top in something. They had caught up well with the rest of their form, but as most of the other girls had been there a good deal longer than they had, Miss Roberts told them that they could not expect to come out top that term.

The maths. exam. came first. It was quite a stiff one, for Miss Roberts had taught her form a good deal that term and expected them to make a good showing. Pat and Isabel groaned over it, but did their best.

"I know I got questions 3, 4 and 5 quite wrong," said Isabel, when they compared their papers afterwards. "I think I got the problems right though, but they took me so long to puzzle out that I didn't do them all."

"I bet I'll be bottom," said Pat, dismally. She still at times resented being a "nobody", as she put it, though she was rapidly forgetting all the high-and-mighty ideas she had held at first.

French wasn't so bad. Thanks to "Mam'zelle Abominable's" coaching the twins were now well up to the average of their class in writing. It was poor Doris who "fell down" in French. She stammered and stuttered in the oral exam. and drove Mam'zelle nearly frantic.

"Have I taught you three terms already and still you speak French like a four-year-old in the kindergarten?" she stormed. "Now repeat to me again one of the French verses you learnt this term."

The crosser Mam'zelle got, the worse poor Doris became. She gazed hopelessly round the class, and winked at the twins.

"Ah! You wink! You will soon wink the other side of your face!" cried Mam'zelle, getting all mixed up. "You will have nought for your oral French."

As Doris had expected to be bottom anyhow this did not disturb her a great deal. She sat down thankfully. Joan was next, and as she was good at French, Mam'zelle calmed down a little.

The exams. went on until only the geography one was left. The twins examined the lists each morning and were sad to see that they were not top in anything at all. They were not even second in anything! Pat managed to get third in nature, and Isabel fifth in history, but that was the highest they reached!

"Golly! Our exam. marks won't look too good on our reports," sighed Pat. "We were always top in most things at Redroofs, long before we were head of the school. Mother and Daddy won't like us not being top in a single thing here."

"They'll think we did what we said, and didn't try at all," said Isabel. "Oh, blow! And we have been trying. What a pity we said all we did before we came. I don't see how Daddy can help feeling we've slacked all this term. He's so used to getting reports that show us top in nearly everything."

"Well – there's only the geography exam. left," said Pat. "We might be top in that – but I doubt it! I don't feel I know an awful lot about Africa, though we've been studying the wretched place all term. Which part of it do the Zulus live? I never can remember."

"I wish we *could* just be top in it," said Isabel, getting out her geography text-book, and turning over the pages. "Pat – let's cram hard all tonight and really see if we can't do well. Come on!"

So the two of them bent their heads over their text-books and solemnly began to read through the whole of the lessons they had had that term on Africa. They looked at the maps they had drawn, and drew them roughly again two or three times. They made lists of towns and ports and said them to one another. They pored over the rivers and learnt those too, and read up about the peoples of Africa, the animals and the products.

"Well, I really feel I know something now," said Isabel, with a sigh. "I especially know all the products of Africa, and the rivers."

"And I especially know all about the climate," said Pat. "But I bet we shan't get asked questions about those things! Exam. questions always seem to deal with the things you missed because you were ill, or forgot to look up, or for some reason simply can't remember at all!"

"Well, I can't do any more work tonight," said Isabel. "I want to finish the sleeve of the jumper I'm knitting. I've only got a few more rows to do. Where did I put the pattern book?"

"Can't imagine," said Pat. "You're always losing it. I think you took it into the form-room with you this afternoon."

"Blow!" said Isabel. "So I did."

She got up and went out of the common room. She quite forgot that she and the others had been told not to go to the first form room that evening, because the exam.

139

papers were to be set out there. She sauntered along to the room, opened the door and went in. She walked over to her desk and opened it.

Yes – there was the pattern-book. Good! Isabel took it, and then picked up a pencil that belonged to Miss Roberts. She went to the teacher's big desk and put it in the groove that held pencils and pens.

And there, staring up at her from the desk were the exam. papers for tomorrow! A list of geography questions was written out very neatly on a sheet of paper. Isabel stared at them with a beating heart.

If only she knew what the questions were she could cram them up and answer them so perfectly that she would be top! Without thinking she hurriedly read down the questions. "State what you know about the climate of South Africa. What do you know about the race called Pygmies? What do you . . ."

Isabel read the questions from top to bottom, and then went out of the room. Her face was flushed and her heart was beating. "All those questions are what we've both been looking up this evening," she said to herself. "It doesn't matter me seeing the paper at all. I've already crammed up the answers."

Pat looked up as Isabel came back into the common room. "Got the pattern book?" she asked.

Isabel looked down at her empty hands. No – she had left the pattern book behind after all.

"Didn't you find it?" said Pat, surprised.

"Yes – I did," said Isabel. "But I've gone and left it behind after all."

"Well, aren't you going to go and get it?" asked Pat, still more surprised. Isabel hesitated. She could not bear to go back into the form room again.

"What *is* the matter, Isabel?" asked Pat, impatiently. "Have you gone dumb? What's up?"

"Pat, the geography paper questions were on Miss

Roberts' desk," said Isabel. "I read them."

"Isabel! That's cheating!" said Pat.

"I didn't think about whether it was cheating or not," said Isabel, in a troubled voice. "But it's all right, Pat – the questions were all about what we've been looking up this evening. So it won't matter."

Pat stared at Isabel. Isabel would not look at her. "Isabel, I don't see how in the world you're going to sit for the geography exam. tomorrow when you know you've already seen the questions," she said at last. "I dare say you could answer them all quite perfectly without any further looking up at all – but if any one knew about this they'd think you were a cheat. And you're not – you've always been straight and honourable. I just don't understand you."

"I did it all in a hurry," said poor Isabel.

"Well, you'd better tell Miss Roberts," said Pat.

"Oh, I *can't*!" said Isabel, in horror. "You know how strict she is. I can't."

"Well, you must answer all the questions so badly that Miss Roberts will be angry with you, and then you can tell her why you've done it," said Pat. "If she knows you haven't taken advantage of seeing the questions she can't think you're a cheat. You'll have to own up before or after. Go on now, Isabel, you know you must."

"Well – I'll own up afterwards," said Isabel. "I'll sit for the exam. and do the answers so badly that I'll be bottom. Then when Miss Roberts rows me I'll tell her why. Oh, blow! Why was I so silly? I did it all in a hurry. I might even have been top, you know – because all the questions were ones I could answer quite well."

"Don't tell me what they were," said Pat. "I don't want to know, else I'll feel awkward about answering them. Cheer up, Isabel, I know you well enough to know you didn't mean to cheat! Anybody can be silly!"

141

Isabel was not very happy that night. She tossed and turned, wishing to goodness she hadn't seen the geography questions. She could so easily have answered them correctly and got high marks! What an idiot she had been!

The geography exam. was to be held first thing after prayers next day. At nine o'clock all the first form filed into their room, and took their places. Isabel saw that the exam questions were still on the desk. Pat saw them there too, though of course it was impossible for any one to read them.

Miss Roberts came in. "Good morning, girls!" she said. "Good morning, Miss Roberts," chorused the class, and sat down.

"Geography exam. this morning," said Miss Roberts, briskly. "Do well, please! Joan, come and give out the questions."

Isabel watched Joan go up for the slips of paper. She felt miserable. It was not nice to have to do badly on purpose, but there was nothing else to do.

Just as Joan was taking up the papers Miss Roberts gave an exclamation and stopped her. "Wait! I don't believe these are the right papers! No – they're not! How stupid! They are the exam. questions for the second form, who have been doing Africa too. Go to Miss Jenks with these, and ask her to give you the papers I left on her desk. Tell her I've left the first form's exam. questions there, and that these are for her form."

Joan took the papers and disappeared out of the room. Isabel looked at Pat. Pat was smiling in delight. When Miss Roberts turned to write something on the board Pat leaned across and whispered to Isabel.

"What luck! Now you can do your best instead of your worst, old girl! You saw the wrong questions! Hurrah!"

Isabel nodded. She was really delighted too. It seemed

142

too good to be true. Miss Roberts turned round. "No talking! If I catch any girls whispering during exams. I shall deduct ten marks from their papers. Do you hear me, Pat?"

"Yes, Miss Roberts," said Pat, meekly. Joan came back with the right papers and distributed them round the class. Isabel read hers quickly. Yes – they were quite, quite different from the questions she had read last night. How marvellous! Now she could set to work and really do her best to be top. She would never be such an idiot again. She hadn't meant to be a cheat, but it was horrible to feel like one.

But poor Isabel was rather nervous now after her experiences, and did not do nearly such a good paper as Pat. Her hand shook as she drew the maps required, and she made some silly mistakes. So when the papers were gathered up and corrected Isabel was nowhere near the top! She was sixth – but Pat was top! Isabel was as pleased to see Pat's name heading the list as she would have been to see her own. She squeezed her twin's arm hard.

"Good for you, Pat!" she said. "I'm jolly glad! One of us is top in something anyhow!"

Pat glowed with pleasure. It was marvellous to see her name heading the list. Miss Roberts came up and patted her on the back.

"You did an excellent paper, Patricia," she said. "Eighty-three per cent is very good. But I was surprised that Isabel didn't do better? Why was that, Isabel?"

But Isabel did not tell her and Miss Roberts laughed and went on her way. Surprising things happened in exams. – probably next term those O'Sullivan twins would be top in nearly everything!

And now the end of the term was indeed drawing near. Miss Theobald and the other mistresses were busy making out reports, putting up lists, helping the girls with the great concert, and going through exam. papers. The girls themselves were restless, looking forward to the holidays, getting ready for the concert, wondering what their reports would be like, and nearly driving Mam-'zelle mad with their inattention.

Miss Roberts was more lenient, but even she grew impatient when Isabel told her that there were fourteen ounces in a pound.

"I know you all go *slightly* mad at the end of term," she said, "but there really is a limit to my patience. Isabel, if there was a lower form than this I'd send you to it for the rest of the morning!"

The last two weeks were really great fun. For one thing all the cupboards had to be turned out, washed, dried and tidied. The twins had never done this at Redroofs School, and at first were inclined to turn up their noses at such work. But when they saw the others tying handkerchiefs round their hair, and putting on overalls, they couldn't help thinking it would be rather fun, even though the cleaning had to be done in their free time.

"Come on, Pat, come on, Isabel! Don't stand looking stuck-up like you used to!" cried Janet, who sensed at once the twins hadn't done work like this before. "You'll get dirty, but you can always bath and wash your hair! Come on, high-and-mighties!"

This was not a name that the twins liked at all, so they climbed down at once. They found big hankies and tied up their hair. They put on overalls, and went to join the others. Hilary was in charge of the first-form cleaning.

It really was fun. Everything had to be taken out of the cupboards, and there were squeals and shrieks of delight when things long-lost came to light again.

"Oh! I thought I'd never see that penknife again!" squealed Doris, pouncing on a small pearl-handled knife in delight. "Wherever has it been all this time?"

"Golly! Here's Miss Roberts' fountain-pen!" cried Hilary, a little later. "Look – tangled up in this bundle of raffia. Oooh! I know how it got there. Do you remember, Janet, when you dumped a whole lot of it on to Miss Roberts' desk in handwork one day, and she objected, and you carted it all off to the cupboard again? Well, I bet you took the pen with you! My word, what a hunt we had for it."

"Well, for pity's sake don't remind her that it might have been *me*," said Janet. "She's always going off the deep end about something now. Look – take her the pen, Isabel, and say we found it in the handwork cupboard. You've been in her bad books today, so maybe you'll get an unexpected smile!"

Isabel did! Miss Roberts was delighted to see her pen, and beamed at Isabel with pleasure. Isabel wondered if Miss Roberts was in a good enough temper to be asked something. She tried.

"Miss Roberts! I'm so sorry I made a mess of my maths. this morning. If I promise to do better tomorrow, need I do those sums all over again? I've such a lot to do today."

But Miss Roberts was not to be caught like that! "My dear Isabel!" she said, "I am delighted that you have been able to give me back my pen – but I think you'll agree with me that that isn't any real reason why I should forgive you for shockingly bad work! And even if you find me my best hat, which unaccountably flew from my head last Sunday and completely disappeared over the fields, I should still say you must do your sums again!"

The class chuckled. Miss Roberts could be very dry when she liked. Isabel laughed too and went back to the cleaning and tidying.

"I wish I *could* find her hat for her!" she said. "She's jolly strict, but she's an awful sport!"

There was great excitement when the night of the concert came. For the last few days before the concert the girls had been in a state of great excitement, getting their lines perfect, and rehearsing everything. Each form was to do something, and the concert was to last three hours, with a break in between for refreshments.

Mam'zelle had taught French plays and songs to each form, and pestered the girls continually to make sure that they were word perfect. The sixth form were doing a short Greek play. The fifth were doing an absurd sketch that they had written themselves, called "Mrs. Jenkins Pays a Call", and borrowed all kinds of queer hats and clothes from the mistresses, and even from the school cook!

The fourth form had got up a jazz band, which sounded simply marvellous, though Mam'zelle said that she could easily do without the side-drum, which could be heard rat-a-tat-tatting from a music room at all kinds of odd hours. The third form were doing part of a Shakespeare play, and the second and first were doing plays and odd things such as Doris's solo dance, and Tessie's recitations.

Sheila was tremendously excited. She knew that if she had been given a part in the history play at the beginning she would never have had the chance of such a big part. Now, because of Vera's accident, she had a fine part. She practised it continually, thinking about it, putting in

146

actions that Vera had never thought of, and astonishing every one by her acting.

"She's going to be jolly good!" whispered Janet to Pat. "I'm quite getting to like old Sheila now. Who would have thought there was a hardworking, interesting little person like that underneath all those old posings and boastings of hers!"

Pat and Isabel worked their hardest for the concert too. All the mistresses and the staff were coming and the whole school would be watching. Nobody must forget their words or do anything silly. Each form had its own honour to uphold!

The great night came. There were gigglings and whisperings all day long. Lessons slacked off that day, except Mam'zelle's French classes. Mam'zelle would surely not allow even an earthquake to spoil her lessons! No wonder that the girls were such excellent French scholars by the time that they reached the top form.

The sewing mistress worked at top speed to alter dresses at the last moment. Matron proved unexpectedly good at providing a real meal in one of the plays, instead of the pretend-one that Hilary had arranged for.

"Golly! Isn't that decent of her!" said Hilary, looking at the jug of lemonade and the currant buns that Matron had presented her with. "I *shall* enjoy my part in the play now!"

"Well, don't stuff your mouth so full that you can't speak," grinned Janet. "I say – what about asking Mam'zelle to let us have a meal of some sort in the French play too."

But nobody dared to mention such a thing to Mam'zelle!

At six o'clock the concert began. Everyone had filed into the gym., where benches and chairs had been set ready. The stage had its curtains and footlights, and looked fine. There were pots of plants borrowed from Miss Theobald's hothouse at the sides.

The mistresses sat in the three front rows leaving their forms to look after themselves for once. The kitchen staff sat behind the mistresses. The girls were on benches at the back, completely filling the gym.

Everyone had a programme, designed and coloured by the girls themselves. Pat was terribly proud to see that Miss Theobald had the one that she herself had done. She saw the Head looking carefully at the design of the cover, and she wondered if Miss Theobald would see her name in the corner – Pat O'Sullivan.

Every form knew when its turn was coming and knew when it must rise quietly and go to the back of the stage to dress and await its turn. The fifth form were acting their play first, and as soon as the curtains swung aside and showed the girls dressed up most ridiculously in odd hats and coats and shawls, the audience went off into fits of laughter. The school cook squealed out, "Oh, there's my old hat! I never thought I'd see it on a stage!"

The sketch was really funny and the audience loved it. Then came the Greek play by the sixth which was really a serious and difficult thing to understand. The first-formers listened politely and clapped hard at the end, but they secretly thought that the fifth form were very much better!

The fourth form came on with their jazz band, and this was an instant success. The drummer was simply marvellous and Mam'zelle quite forgave the constant irritation that the practising of the drum had given her. Swinging dance tunes were played, and the audience roared the choruses. They kept clapping for encores, but as it was now half-time, the jazz band had to stop at last!

How the girls enjoyed the trifles and jellies, cream-buns, sandwiches and lemonade! When they went into the dining-room to have their meal, they gasped at the sight of so much food.

"Golly! We'll never, never eat all that!" cried Pat.

"Patricia O'Sullivan, you don't know what you're talking about!" said Janet, lifting up a plate of asparagus sandwiches. "Speak for yourself! Have one – or two whilst they're here."

And sure enough Pat didn't know what she was talking about – for in twenty minutes not a thing was left on the dishes! The girls made a clean sweep of everything – and, hidden under the long cloth of the table, sat some one as hungry as the girls – Binks, the puppy-dog!

Kathleen had let him out secretly and had tied him to a leg of the big table. She gave him bits of sausage roll, which he ate eagerly. He was sensible enough not to poke his nose out in case he was discovered, and nobody guessed he was there except Isabel, who had been filled with astonishment at the amount of sausage rolls that Kathleen was apparently able to eat.

Then she suddenly realized what was happening. "Oh – you monkey, Kath! You've got Binks there."

"Sh!" said Kathleen. "Don't say a word. I didn't see why he should miss the fun. Isn't he good?"

Binks had a marvellous time after that, for there were two people feeding him instead of one!

The concert began again in half an hour. The first form gave their two short plays, and Sheila acted so magnificently that the audience actually roared her name and made her come and give a special bow. The girl was happier than ever she had been in her life, and looked quite pretty as she stood on the stage, flushed and excited. Winifred, the head-girl, smiled across at Pat to let her know how pleased she was, for she guessed that Pat and the others had been giving Sheila the chance she had begged for her.

The French play was a success too, and Mam'zelle

beamed round with pleasure when she heard it clapped so heartily. "Those first-form kids aren't half bad," Isabel heard Belinda Towers say, and she stored it up in her mind to tell the others later on.

Doris did her dance, which was really excellent. She too was encored, and came on again in a clown's dress. She proceeded to do the clown dance which had ended so disastrously on the night of the Great Feast, and this time it ended in plenty of cheers and clapping. Just as she was finishing, a disturbance arrived in the shape of Binks!

He had bitten through his lead and had come to join his mistress. Kathleen was in the wings at the side of the stage, watching Doris dancing. Binks leapt up on to the stage joyfully, to join Kathleen, and tripped Doris up very neatly, for all the world as if he were joining in the dance!

Doris promptly fell over just as the music ended. How the audience laughed and cheered! Binks turned round as he heard them, his pink tongue hanging out, and his tail wagging joyfully. Then he went to Kathleen, who, fearful of being scolded, rushed off at once to put him back into the stables.

But nobody scolded her, not even Mam'zelle, who had never ceased to say that she thought it was "abominable" and "insupportable" to allow "that dog" in the school!

The concert ended with the whole school singing the school song, a very swinging, heartening tune that the twins heard for the first time. They were the only ones who did not know it.

"We'll sing it *next* time!" whispered Pat to Isabel. "Oh, Isabel! What a lovely evening! It beats Redroofs hollow, don't you think?"

Then yawning hugely, for it was an hour past their usual bedtime, the first-formers went up to bed. They chattered and laughed as they undressed, and were just as long as they liked – for this was the last evening of term, and tomorrow they were breaking up and going home!

The Last Day

Next day the trunks were dragged down from the loft. Each had its owner's name on in white paint, and soon they were being packed. Matron bustled to and fro, giving out clothes, and seeing that the girls packed at least moderately well. She made Doris take out every single thing and begin again.

"But Matron, I'll never have time!" said Doris laughing at Matron's annoyed face.

"If you stay here till next week you will pack properly!" said Matron, grimly. "Doris Elward, your mother and your two aunts came here years ago, and they never learnt to pack – but *you* are going to! It is *not* sensible to put breakable things at the bottom of your trunk, and shoes and boots on the top of your best things. Begin again!"

"Kath! What's your home address?" yelled Pat. "You said you'd give it to me and you haven't. I want to write to you for Christmas."

Kathleen went red with pleasure. No one had even bothered to ask for her address before. She wrote it down for Pat. Then there was a general exchange of addresses, and promises to telephone, and invitations for parties after Christmas if so-and-so could only manage to come

The school didn't seem like school any more. Everywhere there was babbling and chattering and giggling, and even when mistresses came into the classrooms

151

and dormitories nobody thought of being quiet. The mistresses were excited too, and talked laughingly among themselves.

"I'm pleased with my lot this term," said Miss Roberts, watching Sheila throw something across to Pat. "Two or three of them have altered so much for the better that I hardly know them."

"What about those O'Sullivan twins?" asked Miss Jenks. "I thought they were going to be a handful when they came. They were called the 'stuck-up twins', you know, and at first I couldn't bear the look of their discontented faces."

"Oh, they're all right," said Miss Roberts at once. "They've settled down well. They've got good stuff in them. One of these days St. Clare's will be proud of them, mark my words! They're monkeys, though. Look out when you get them in your form some time next year!"

"Oh, they'll be all right after a term or two in your tender care!" laughed Miss Jenks. "I never have any trouble with girls that come up into my form from yours. It's only the new girls that come straight into my form that I have bother with."

Mam'zelle sailed by, beaming. She always entered every girl's address in a little black holiday note-book, and most conscientiously wrote to every one of them in the holidays.

"Good old 'Mam'zelle Abominable'!" whispered Pat as she went by. Mam'zelle's sharp ears heard what she said.

"What is that you call me?" she demanded, towering over Pat as she knelt packing her trunk.

"Oh – nothing, Mam'zelle," said Pat, horror-struck to think that Mam'zelle might have overheard. The other girls looked round, grinning. They all knew the twins' name for Mam'zelle.

"You will tell me, please. I demand it!" insisted Mam'zelle, her eyes beginning to flash.

"Well," said Pat, reluctantly, "I only call you 'Mam'zelle Abominable' because at first you called me and Isabel and our work abominable so often. Please don't be cross!"

But Mam'zelle was not cross. For some reason the name tickled her sense of humour, and she threw back her head and roared.

"Ha! 'Mam'zelle Abominable'! That is a fine name to call your French mistress. And next term your work will be so fine that I shall say you are *magnifique!* and you will then call me 'Mam'zelle Magnifique', *n'est ce pas?*"

At last all the packing was done. Each girl went to say a polite good-bye to Miss Theobald. When the twins went in together, she looked at them seriously, and then smiled an unusually sweet smile at them.

"I don't think you wanted to come to St. Clare's, did you?" she said. "And now somehow I think you've changed your minds?"

"Yes, we *have* changed our minds!" said Pat honestly. She never minded owning up when she altered her ideas. "We hated coming here. We were going to be really awful, and we did try to be. But – well – St. Clare's is fine."

"And we shall simply *love* coming back again next term," said Isabel, eagerly. "It's hard work here, and things aren't a bit the same as at our old school, and it's odd being one of the young ones after being top of the school – but we've got used to it now."

"One day maybe you'll be one of the top ones at St. Clare's," said Miss Theobald.

But the thought of being as grand and great as Winifred James was too much for the twins. "Oh, no!" said Pat. "We could never, never be that!"

But Miss Theobald smiled a secret smile. She knew far more about the girls than they knew about themselves, and she felt sure that she was right. These troublesome twins had the makings of fine girls, and she and St. Clare's would see to it that they fulfilled the promise they showed.

"Here are your reports," she said, and gave one to each girl. "Give my love to your mother and tell her that I haven't had to expel you yet!"

"I hope our reports are good," said Pat. "We told Daddy we weren't going to try a bit – and if they're bad he'll think we were jolly mean."

"Well, you'll see when you get home!" said Miss Theobald, smiling. "But – I wouldn't worry very much if I were you! Good-bye!"

The twins said good-bye to every one, and received fat kisses on each cheek from Mam'zelle, who seemed unaccountably fond of every girl that day. Miss Roberts shook hands and warned them not to eat too much plum pudding. Miss Kennedy looked rather sad as she said good-bye, for her friend, Miss Lewis, was now quite well, and was coming back to take up her old post the next term.

"I shan't see you again," said Kenny, as she said good-bye to the twins. "I'm going to miss you all very much."

"Good-bye, Kenny," said Pat. "We were pigs to you at first – but you do forgive us for being piggy, don't you? And I do promise to write. I won't forget."

"Neither will I," said Isabel, and then Janet and Hilary and the rest came crowding up, and Miss Kennedy grew quite tearful as the girls poured good-byes and good wishes on her. What a good thing it was that she hadn't been a failure after all!

The most uproarious person that day was Binks. He was set free and spent his time taking chocolate from

154

his friends, and going round licking people's hands and faces as they knelt to pack. No mistress had the heart to complain about him and he had a marvellous time.

"He *will* hate leaving me when I come back to school again!" said Kathleen, as she patted his wiry head. "But never mind – we shall have a whole month together. Miss Theobald wrote to my aunt, and Aunt is going to see if he behaves."

"Of *course* he'll behave!" said Janet. "But I expect he'll take after you, Kathleen – sometimes he'll behave well – and sometimes he won't!"

Kathleen laughed and gave Janet an affectionate punch. She didn't live a great way from the twins and they had already made plans to cycle over and see one another. She was very happy.

The bell rang to say that the first coach was ready to take the girls to the station. That was for the first form. Shouting good-byes to their teachers, the girls ran helter-skelter down the stairs and piled into the big motor-coach. What fun to be breaking up! What fun to be going home to Christmas jollities, parties and theatres! There were Christmas presents to buy, Christmas cards to send, all kinds of things to look forward to.

Pat and Isabel got into the train together and sat down with the others to wait for the rest of the school to come down in the coaches. Before very long the engine gave a violent whistle and the carriages jerked. They were off!

The twins craned their heads out of the window to see the last of the big white building they had grown to love.

"Good-bye!" said Pat under her breath. "We hated you when we first saw you, St. Clare's! But now we love you!"

"And we'll be glad to see you again!" whispered Isabel. "Oh, Pat – it's marvellous that we'll be going back

155

in four weeks' time, isn't it? Good old St. Clare's!"

And then the school disappeared from sight, and the train rattled on its noisy way, singing a song that seemed to say over and over again, "We're pleased we're coming back again-TO-ST.-CLARE'S! We're pleased we're coming back again TO-ST.-CLARE'S!"

A funny song, but quite a true one, thought the twins!

THE ENID BLYTON TRUST
FOR CHILDREN

We hope you have enjoyed the adventures of the children in this book. Please think for a moment about those children who are too ill to do the exciting things you and your friends do.

Help them by sending a donation, large or small to the ENID BLYTON TRUST FOR CHILDREN. The Trust will use all your gifts to help children who are sick or handicapped and need to be made happy and comfortable.

Please send your postal orders or cheques to:

> The Enid Blyton Trust for Children,
> International House
> 1 St Katharine's Way
> London E1 9UN

Thank you very much for your help.

Have you read all the adventures in the "Mystery" series by Enid Blyton?

The Rockingdown Mystery

Roger, Diana, Snubby and Barney hear strange noises in the cellar while staying at Rockingdown Hall. Barney goes to investigate and makes a startling discovery . . .

The Rilloby Fair Mystery

Valuable papers have disappeared – the Green Hands Gang has struck again! Which of Barney's workmates at the circus is responsible? The four friends turn detectives – and have to tackle a dangerous criminal.

The Ring O'Bells Mystery

Eerie things happen at deserted Ring O'Bells Hall – bells start to ring, strange noises are heard in a secret passage, and there are some very unfriendly strangers about. Something very mysterious is going on and the friends mean to find out what . . .

The Rubadub Mystery

Who is the enemy agent at the top-secret submarine harbour? Roger, Diana, Snubby and Barney are determined to find out – and find themselves involved in a most exciting mystery.

The Rat-A-Tat Mystery

When the big knocker on the ancient door of Rat-A-Tat House bangs by itself in the middle of the night, it heralds a series of very peculiar happenings – and provides another action-packed adventure for Roger, Diana, Snubby and Barney.

The Ragamuffin Mystery

"This is going to be the most exciting holiday we've ever had," said Roger – and little does he know how true his words will prove when he and his three friends go to Merlin's Cove and discover the hideout of a gang of thieves.

Armada

Have you read all the "Secrets" stories by Enid Blyton?

THE SECRET ISLAND

Peggy, Mike and Nora are having a miserable time with unkind Aunt Harriet and Uncle Henry – until they make friends with wild Jack and discover the secret island.

THE SECRET OF SPIGGY HOLES

On a holiday by the sea, Mike, Jack, Peggy and Nora discover a secret passage – and a royal prisoner in a sinister cliff-top house. The children plan to free the young prince – and take him to the secret island.

THE SECRET MOUNTAIN

Jack, Peggy, Nora and Mike team up with Prince Paul of Baronia to search for their parents, who have been kidnapped and taken to the secret mountain. Their daring rescue mission seems doomed to failure – especially when the children are captured and one of them is to be sacrificed to the sun-god.

THE SECRET OF KILLIMOOIN

When Prince Paul invited Nora, Mike, Peggy and Jack to spend the summer holidays with him in Baronia, they were thrilled. By amazing luck, they find the hidden entrance to the Secret Forest – but can they find their way out?

THE SECRET OF MOON CASTLE

Moon Castle is said to have had a violent, mysterious past so Jack, Peggy, Mike and Nora are wildly excited when Prince Paul's family rent it for the holidays. When weird things begin to happen, the children are determined to know the strange secrets the castle hides . . .

Armada

THE MYSTERY THAT NEVER WAS
by

Enid Blyton

Don't miss this exciting adventure story by the world's best-ever storyteller!

Nicky decides to invent a mystery for his Uncle Bob — a private investigator — to solve. But there's a nasty shock in store for Nicky. When spooky lights signal in the night from the old mansion on Skylark Hill, he realises that his mystery is coming horrifyingly true.

Armada